The War is Over

MENDING SHATTERED HEARTS #2

NIKKI A LAMERS

For more information, address: freydreamspublications@gmail.com

First paperback edition was included in part of Wreck My Halls, November 2024

First full paperback edition, June 2025

Editor, Dina Huessini

ISBN 978-1-951185-31-2 (paperback)

ISBN 978-1-951185-30-5 (ebook)

www.nikkialamersauthor.com

Other Books By Nikki A Lamers

All books are standalone novels, except the first two books in the Home Series.

The Unforgettable Series

The Unforgettable Summer (#1)
Unforgettable Nights (#2)
Unforgettable Dreams (#3)
Unforgettable Memories (#4)
The Unforgettable One (#5)

NIKKI A LAMERS

Unforgettable Mistakes (#6)
An Unforgettable December Novella (#7)

Home

Dreams Lost and Found (#1)
Finding Home (#2)

Mending Shattered Hearts

Breaking Cycles (#1)
The War is Over Novella (#2)
Breaking Barriers (#3)

Piper Falls: Station 28

Leave of My Duty (#5)

Love Canyon: Blind Date with a #BOOKBOYFRIEND

Blind Date with a #FORMERPLAYER (November 2025)

Waves Crashing

The Lost Princess Prequel (Coming 2025)

Chapter 1

Sloane

"Ugh! I can't believe you're dragging me out," I complain, trudging across the gravel parking lot towards a local dive bar on the edge of town.

"I'm not dragging you. You're walking on your own two feet."

My pale blue eyes narrow at my best friend, Alex. "Not willingly."

She huffs a laugh. "Now we both know that's not true. If you really didn't want to come, you would be at your apartment sitting on the couch with a tub of mint chocolate chip ice cream watching Christmas movies and waiting to meet your new roommate."

I scrunch up my nose. "Yeah, no Christmas movies." I turn away from her and keep walking, knowing she's mostly right.

She winces and wobbles in her heels, grabbing my arm so she doesn't fall. We probably look like we're already wasted. "Sorry, Sloane."

I wave her off like it's no big deal. It's not that I don't like Christmas, but it's definitely not my favorite time of year like most of the world. Unfortunately, that has more to do with my family than anything else.

"Look, my point is you're the one who's been a scrooge lately and I don't get to come visit you and my brother all the time, but I'm here. That's why you're not backing out and we're walking through that door and onto that sticky beer-soaked wood floor."

"Sounds fabulous," I mutter, frowning. She yanks on the door handle, the smell of stale beer and sweat hitting my nostrils. "Why is this a good idea?" Alex glares at me out of the corner of her eye. Groaning, I concede, "Fine. I've got my big girl panties on. I'm ready."

At my words, a handsome unfamiliar man halts his conversation with Pax, the bouncer, and turns his head towards me. His green eyes roam my body, looking me up and down from head to toe sending a shiver down my spine. I stand a little straighter, confident in my dark blue jeans and pale blue body suit with a scoop neck showcasing my chest. Most would say I'm blessed with my breasts, but there's so much more to me than my girls.

The man leans against the wall, likely about six feet tall with broad shoulders, dark, wavy, brown hair, a killer smile, and a five-o-clock shadow that I'm sure would feel incredible between my legs. He stares at me, sipping the drink in his hand causing me to arch my eyebrows in challenge. "May I help you?"

"Big girl panties? What do those look like?" His deep, sexy voice rumbles over my skin as my body heats instantly with embarrassment.

"Do you always eavesdrop on other people's conversations?"

He chuckles, his eyes alight with amusement as he stares at me. "I'm just standing near the door and lucky me, you two walk inside talking about your panties. So, can I see them?"

A gasp leaves my lips. "No, you can't."

His lips curve up in a cocky grin, his tongue slipping out and licking them drawing my attention whether I want it there or not. Pushing off the wall, he steps closer, his voice going low. "Are you sure about that? The night is still young."

"Seriously?"

"Care to make a wager?" he asks, taking another step into my space, towering over me.

My breathing picks up as I look up at this gorgeous man and I quickly try to reign in my thoughts, along with my body's reaction. "I'm not betting you anything."

"So, you already know I'll have you in my bed by the end of the night." He grins wide, the look taking my breath away.

Shaking my head, I put my hand up to keep him at bay, but the moment I touch him, my fingers tingle. I bite my lower lip to keep myself from saying something stupid. This sexy, egotistical man is the last thing I need. "No."

"Isn't that why you came out with me?" Alex asks, arching her brow.

Gasping, my eyes widen as I turn, looking at my ex best friend with pure disbelief. She shrugs, non-apologetic. "Not helping and no. I came because I never get to see you. Besides, I didn't think there would be anyone new in town."

"Well, there is and it's not me he's interested in." Alex wiggles her eyebrows suggestively and giggles, clearly amused.

He's jostled from behind and steps into me, grabbing my waist so he doesn't crash into me. Surprising myself, I don't step back. I stare into his captivating emerald eyes, but he quickly opens his mouth and ruins the moment. "I knew I'd have you in my arms before the end of the night."

Pressing my lips together, I push at his chest, and he releases me. Laughing, he holds his hands up as if he's innocent when he's anything but. "I'm just having fun. You're absolutely gorgeous."

I look at him out of the corner of my eye, unsure if I should trust him. This man has devil written all over him. Pushing my dark blonde hair behind my ears, I warily mumble, "Thanks."

"Sorry about that." Gordon apologizes to the man for bumping into him, looking sheepish. He grins at us. "Hey, Alex, Sloane. How's it going?"

Before I get a chance to respond, the stranger clears his throat, interrupting. "What's up?"

Gordon looks at him and gives a slight shake of his head. "Just wanted to give you a heads up. Meg was looking for you."

Frowning, I step past him, waving to Gordon, Alex following right behind as we head for the bar. "See you, later, Gordon," she calls over her shoulder.

I grew up with him, but he's two years older than me, the same age as my brother, Jake. Alex and I got close in high school. She graduated from here, but she didn't always go to our school.

I lean over the oak bar, already decorated for Christmas. A bowl of ornaments sits in the middle. Garland wrapped with colored lights is draped around the bottles and glasses. A few hand painted wine bottles filled with lights and tinsel stand out, adding to the decorations on the shelves in place of alcohol filled bottles. "Hey, Lucy." I smile at the redhead.

She grins, bouncing over to us, her red ponytail swinging behind her. Lucy has always had more energy than anyone I've known. She works hard, supporting her younger brothers since her mom has been sick and out of work for as long as I can remember.

"Hey, y'all! How have you been?"

"Good," we both answer.

"It's been a while since I've seen you, Alex. How's your brother?"

"He's good. Working hard to get his new shop running with his partner."

"Yeah, I've heard some good things about G & A's Cycles Specialty Shop already."

Alex smiles. "That's great to hear. And, since he's so busy, I thought I'd come visit him and as a bonus, I finally got this one to come out with me." Alex thrusts her thumb in my direction.

"I've been...busy."

Both of them laugh, Lucy smirking as she looks at me. "He's not here if you're wondering."

I breathe a sigh of relief, my body sagging into the bar. "Thanks. I don't care, but I don't want to deal with him. Not yet."

"I get it. It's never easy to break up around here, no matter how long it's been, you always run into them," Lucy comments, giving me a look of empathy.

"The hazards of living in a small beach town." I nod, although in my situation, that's only a small part of it. "How's your mom?"

Pasting a smile on her face, Lucy claims, "She's good. Thanks. What can I get you two?"

"Whatever light beer you have on tap is fine."

She nods and comes back moments later setting two pint glasses in front of us while I place a twenty on the bar. "Thank you," Alex and I say in unison.

"So—why not him? He's sexy as hell."

My eyes drift to the stranger, standing with his arms crossed over his chest, making his muscles bulge as he dangles his glass between his fingertips. "Yeah, he is, but who is he?"

She giggles. "Who cares. Go for it."

"But why is he here? It's not like you see a lot of people moving to Genesis Beach, North Carolina unless you have family here or you've been here before. He must be visiting someone."

"Maybe, but maybe that's exactly what you need; one hot night with a stranger."

"I'm not you."

She shrugs. "But it's so much fun." Her eyes widen, licking her lips as the owner of the bar steps out from the back room. Ace Morgan likely has at least ten years on us. He's six-foot, two with salt and pepper hair, and green eyes. "I'd love to climb that tree."

My lips twitch in amusement as we watch him walk over to the stranger, giving him a firm pat on the back. They obviously know each other. "Keep doing you, girl." I'll never understand how she adores older men, but I don't need to. "If you want to wade in, don't worry about me."

"You need to get back out there so much more than I do."

"I really don't."

"You sure about that? It's not going to bother you seeing Dan and Fiona together?"

I wince at the mention of my ex-fiancé and his new girlfriend, also my stepsister; the same girlfriend he started dating days after we broke up because I wasn't passionate enough. Whatever. "Just because every time I see them, they look like they can't keep their hands off each other or their tongues in their mouths, doesn't mean it will be hard for me to see them."

"I heard they got engaged."

My eyes widen and my mouth drops open, gasping in shock. "What?"

She gives me the same look of sympathy I loathe. "I'm sorry, Sloane. I thought you knew."

"No, but it's fine. It's totally fine. I definitely don't want him, it's just weird. He would be like a step-brother-in-law." Making a face, I shrug. Looking around the room, my eyes catch on the same green-eyed stranger.

A familiar blonde woman sidles up to him, throwing her arms around his neck and kissing him on his cheek, whispering in his ear.

Licking his lips, a slow, easy grin lights up his face. He glances at me, catching my eye before shrugging.

"What an asshole," I mutter under my breath.

"Pretty sure he was just looking to hookup while he's here. Same thing I do. I have a lot of fun with one night stands too. Make me a bitch?"

"No, Alex. Absolutely not." I shake my head in denial.

"Well, then, I have no idea why you wouldn't take him up on it. I mean, look at that man."

"He was a jerk."

"No. He was direct and flirting with you. And you just admitted you thought he was hot so stop pretending you didn't."

Ignoring her comment, I ask, "Wait, was that Margie Harris?"

"Yeah, she moved back last month. She goes by Meg now."

"Ugh," I groan. "I'm too old for this shit."

"Twenty-six is not old."

"You're only saying that because you're a year older than me."

"Ten months, Sloane. Ten. Months."

"Okay, ten months. But I'm not going to hook up with some overbearing, obnoxious, player who has an ego the size of Saturn."

"Sure. And it has nothing to do with the fact that it's been a while? Or that Fiona left town? How about the fact that Dan doesn't have her as a constant appendage this weekend? You didn't think maybe you two could talk so you could finally get some damn closure?"

Grimacing, I drink my beer.

I really am over him, but I thought I was going to marry the guy. The thought of seeing him with her turns my stomach and makes me feel like a damn fool. "No. I want nothing to do with him." Frowning, I look around the room. "But if I'm going to hook up with someone, why can't it be a successful, sexy, smart man who is ready for a real relationship?"

She arches her eyebrows in challenge. "That's the opposite of a one-night stand."

I wave her off, gesturing to the man across the bar. "Well, a guy like that only wants one thing, so he can find it somewhere else. When it comes to sex, I need more than that."

She sighs. "You need to get laid and preferably by someone you haven't known your whole life."

"There's not a lot of men like that around here if you haven't noticed." And I don't know if it would matter if there were.

"We don't know him," she nods towards the same man.

"You're right, but I need to actually move on with someone real. Not some asshole who thinks he can have whatever he wants and won't stick around."

"Don't forget, a lot of people have been coming into town to work on the old Sugartop place."

My head falls back as I burst out laughing. "You mean the Sagerton place?"

"Yeah, that place."

"I wonder what they're going to do with it. It would be a dream come true to be able to do the landscape design at a place like that. The house, the land, it's all gorgeous."

"What do you mean for a place like that? Why not exactly that place? You should put your name in for sure."

"I would do almost anything to get a chance to put a proposal in, but I don't have a clue who to contact or where to even start to look."

"Look into it anyway. They would be lucky to have you. But in the meantime, we need to get you some action."

I shake my head. "No. In the meantime, all I need is my pretty pink vibrator and I'll be good."

"First panties, now vibrators? Are they both pink?" the same deep voice asks right next to my ear eliciting goosebumps.

Alex bites her lip to keep herself from laughing. My face heats to the color of a cherry as I slowly spin on my heel, glaring at the gorgeous stranger wearing the same sexy smirk. "Eavesdropping again?"

"It's a damn good conversation to eavesdrop on, but again, right place, right time." He shrugs, chuckling.

"Sure." Forcing my eyes away from him, I take another sip of my beer.

"I'm confident I can do much better than your pretty pink vibrator. How about we test that theory at my place."

My stupid body tingles at his suggestion. Apparently he's not leaving with Meg. I hate that the idea makes me happy. "Are you always this rude?"

"You brought it up. I'm just being a gentleman and offering to help."

"That's what you call it?" I scoff.

Turning away, I shake my head at Alex. "Obviously this isn't the place that has the kind of men you can bring home with you."

He chuckles under his breath. "You're wrong about that Pixie."

The next moment, he jostles into me from behind, his drink spilling down my back making me scream, "Ah!"

"Watch it asshole," he warns someone behind him.

"What the hell?!" I retort, spinning on my heel and glaring at him.

"I'm so sorry. Someone bumped into me. Let me help you."

He reaches over me, grabbing napkins off the bar and attempting to dry my back, my beer held between us. "Don't worry about it," I grumble, sighing heavily.

"It's in your hair."

"Ugh."

Meg steps into my line of sight, glaring at me from over his shoulder, making my eyebrows draw down in question. Clenching her jaw, she shoves him from behind, pushing him into me and spilling my beer down the front of both of us, but mostly on me as she yells, "Jerk!"

Gasping, I stand in shock, soaked with whiskey on one side and beer on the other, angry tears about to spill over.

He turns with fire in his eyes. "What the hell, Meg?"

Shoving him away from me, I step around him and glare at Meg, a malicious smirk on her lips. "You bitch!" I lunge for her, when suddenly I'm stopped as a strong arm wraps around my waist, pulling me to his hard chest.

"Take it easy, Pixie."

My face heats and my body slouches in defeat. "Let me go. I'm not going to do anything." Slowly, he releases me, and I step away.

He moves towards Meg, while I turn towards Alex. "I'm sorry, Alex, are you good?"

"Yeah, you're going home, aren't you?"

Grimacing, I affirm, "Before anything else goes wrong, I'm leaving." Stalking towards the exit, I wave to her over my shoulder, calling, "I'll see you later."

"Text me when you get home!"

I need a shower. But more than anything, I need to forget about tonight's disaster, especially the sexy stranger. I'm not sure if I should've been pissed at him or thanked him when I left.

Maybe my new roommate, Kelly, is all moved in. It's been a busy day, but I don't want to be rude, especially when she's saving me from having to move back home. I guess she would've texted me if she had any problems. Hopefully, her day went better than mine.

Reaching up, I push my alcohol infused hair out of my face and grimace, wanting to just go to sleep and forget about tonight.

Chapter 2

Sloane

A dull, consistent, knocking pulls me out of a deep sleep, causing my eyes to flutter open. Staring into my dark bedroom, I attempt to pull myself out of the fog and figure out where the sound is coming from. Is someone at the door? Maybe my new roommate left and didn't bring her key. Stretching, I stumble out of bed in a white tank with black and white checkered pajama pants. Not bothering to get dressed, I yank my bedroom door open just as moaning hits my ears from the spare bedroom; my new roommate's bedroom.

My eyes widen as the moaning gets louder, realizing the other sound is more like banging against the wall. Guess Kelly did move in last night and apparently her boyfriend came with her. "Great," I mumble under my breath, wishing I were still asleep. I hope I don't have to listen to that *all* the time. The walls are so thin in my little two-bedroom cottage.

Knowing I'm not going to fall back asleep anytime soon, I trudge out to the kitchen, reaching for a glass and pouring myself some water. With a sigh, I lean against the counter and take a big gulp of water, setting it down next to the sink. The moment I turn around, I come face to face with a petite woman about the same age as me, with soft brown skin and almond eyes wearing nothing but a man's t-shirt.

My gaze goes to hers and I give her a genuine smile while she pinches her lips into a thin line. "I'm sorry, I'm still half asleep. How are you?" I say, attempting to wake myself up. Stepping over to her, I wrap my arms around her in a hug.

"Um, I'm ah fine," she stammers, her hands hanging limply at her sides.

"I'm so sorry I wasn't here when you got here. I had a lot to do, but it's so great to finally meet you." I take a step back, biting my lower lip nervously as she stands staring at me, her eyes narrowed, and eyebrows drawn down.

"This isn't strange at all," she mutters, her sarcasm thick on her tongue.

Releasing my lip, I blurt out another apology, "Sorry, small town and all. We hug everyone."

"I could get on board with that." The deep timbre of his voice rumbles over me, eliciting goose bumps.

My heart stops. I know that voice! It's the same one from earlier at the bar.

Raising my gaze, my body heats instantly. "Oh, um, sorry." My eyes scan the familiar kitchen, looking anywhere but at the man standing shirtless in the doorway.

He chuckles stepping closer. Holding out clothes to the woman standing next to me, he advises, "I brought your things. I'd like my shirt back."

The woman huffs, making me lift my gaze and glance in his direction. My mouth drops open, my thoughts flooding with the possibilities of what I could do with a man like him. He's tall, thin, rigid muscles with a clear eight-pack, dark brown hair going in every direction, likely from her fingers, and emerald-green eyes making me melt; the same eyes staring back at me with pure amusement.

"I'm sorry, I'm Sloane, Kelly's new roommate."

He smirks, shaking my hand. The simple touch sends a shock up my arm, eliciting a gasp from my lips. "I remember you, Pixie."

Gulping hard, I glance at my new roommate, but she's looking at both of us like we've lost it, causing my eyebrows to draw down in confusion.

"You can go now," he states, waving her off, confusing me even more as he flops onto the couch.

My eyes widen when she yanks his shirt off, tossing it at his head before she pulls her clothes on and stalks out the door. "Asshole!" she screams, slamming the door behind her.

Why is she leaving him here at three am? I turn to the man, my breath catching in my throat as he relaxes against the cushions. "Did you two have a fight?" He shakes his head, grinning. "Um, are you her boyfriend or something?"

"Or something," he mumbles, his eyes running over me from head to toe, my traitorous body reacting, reaching its boiling point.

"Well, do you have somewhere to be?"

"Nope."

Exhaling a frustrated breath, I blurt out, "Well, you can't stay here."

Meeting my gaze, he arches his eyebrows in challenge. "Well, that's a problem because I was told I could."

My heart hammers against my ribcage. I can barely be in the same room as this man, there's no way I can endure him being around his girl—whatever she is, all the time. This was a bad idea. "I'll talk to my roommate."

His head falls back in laughter, the light sound making my stomach turn. "Go ahead, but that won't help. He's on my side."

He. Chills run down my spine. "What do you mean?"

I watch his every move as he stands, stalking towards me like I'm his prey. My teeth clamp down on my lower lip, attempting to hold back any visceral sounds. "You're Sloane Douglas." I nod, the sound of my name on his lips eliciting goose bumps. "Nice to meet you. I'm Kelly Travers."

No longer able to hold back, a gasp escapes my lips. "No, no way. You can't be Kelly."

A mischievous sparkle lights up his eyes as his grin grows. "Tell that to my mom. Would you like to see my driver's license?"

"Shit." Reality slams into me, causing my breathing to pick up its pace. "You can't live with me, you're..." I gesture to him dramatically.

He tilts his head to the side, assessing me. "I'm what? Hot?"

My eyes narrow on him. "No, yes, no, I mean...ugh!" He bursts out laughing, fueling my anger. "I thought you were a woman. You should have told me."

"You didn't ask."

"I'm not living with you."

"You're moving out? Where are you going?" He quirks a brow.

"No, you are," I retort, wincing at my childish reaction.

"I'm not going anywhere, Pixie. I just moved in today...well, yesterday." He shrugs.

"But..."

"Like you said, this is a small town. You know better than me, but there's nowhere else to go. I've looked. Rentals are nonexistent in this town. Did that change?"

My heart drops into the pit of my stomach as I glare at this man. He's right. If there was another place for him to go, I'd know about it, but there's nothing. I can't leave him stranded, but that means–ugh. "Fine. You can stay, but don't bring your girlfriends here anymore."

"I don't have any girlfriends, so that won't be a problem." Of course, he doesn't. My eyes narrow on him making him chuckle. "Okay, got it. I'll do my best, but no promises."

Taking a deep breath, I close my eyes, trying to calm my racing heart. Opening my eyes, I look up at Kelly, but he's nothing like the Kelly I pictured. He's not even in the same universe. He's gorgeous trouble.

Then again, maybe he's not.

He's obviously a player. So, no matter how attracted I am to this man, that's not me. Sure, I thought about finding someone to hook up with for a hot second after Dan broke up with me, if only to prove him wrong. I can be passionate. But I can't do it.

"Pixie? You alright there?"

My eyes fly open, connecting with his green eyes once again making my heart skip a beat. "Yeah, just tired from someone waking me up at three am. While you're living here, you need to respect my rules."

Nodding he asks, "What kind of rules?"

"Like put a shirt on."

"But I live here, too, now. Too distracting?" he taunts, stretching his arms above his head.

I roll my eyes, not trusting myself to respond because he's right and I hate lying. "Put the toilet seat down, clean up after yourself, and no changing or adding to any decorations unless I say you can."

He nods, his lips twitching up, clearly amused. "I can do that, but what happens if I break the rules?"

I cross my arms over my chest, pushing my breasts up, and drawing his gaze. My nipples pebble, relishing his attention. Blushing, I quickly cover myself. My stupid traitorous body! "Seriously? Already planning on getting kicked out?"

He barks out another laugh. "This is going to be fun. "Pushing up from the couch, he looks at me, smirking. "I need to get some sleep. Night Pixie."

"Why do you keep calling me that?"

Instead of answering, he smirks, licking his lips. I pinch my lips tightly together, watching him walk by me, raising the hair on my arms with his proximity.

Remaining frozen, I stare after him. Chuckling, he winks at me as he steps into the spare bedroom, shutting the door behind him. Air exits my lungs in a whoosh. Finally, I can breathe again.

I can't believe Kelly is the sexy stranger from the bar. I'm screwed.

Chapter 3

Kelly

My alarm beeps, waking me from a perfect dream. Groaning, my hand runs over my face and my eyes blink open as I shut off the irritating sound.

Wow. That's Sloane? My new roommate? The same woman from the bar who refused to give me the time of day when I was being an ass. But for some reason, I couldn't help myself. She's obviously gorgeous, but the way she looked at me was the opposite of the rejection that came out of her mouth. Made me want to walk the line, so I did. Then, that bitch had to go and ruin it, right after I spilled my whiskey all over Sloane''s back. I felt like shit but now, maybe I can make it up to her. That is if I can stop goading her.

Pushing her buttons is too much fun. Every time I tease her, the spark in her eyes turns to fire. I want more of that Sloane. Hell, that Sloane in my bed would likely be every man's wet dream. I run my hand through my hair and tug at the ends at the thought. She definitely makes my dick twitch.

I won't be living with her forever but might as well take advantage of my time while I can–if she'll let me. Guess I'll find out.

My phone pings with a text. Swiping it off the dresser, I glance at the screen, seeing my mom's name.

Mom

The Christmas party is in two weeks. Your dad and I expect you to be there.

"Good morning to you too," I mumble under my breath wondering if I can figure out a way to get out of it. My parents are assholes. They both care too much about what other people think. It may be different people they're worried about, but it's the same outcome. I have no reason to spend any time with either of my parents. I'll do everything I can to avoid it at all costs.

My phone rings before I even set it down. I glance at the screen, a genuine smile tugging at my lips, immediately swiping to answer. "Hi, Gram."

"Good morning, Kelly, dear. How are you?"

"I'm good. You still up for our lunch date?"

"Of course. I'm looking forward to seeing you. I have a nurse I'd like to introduce you to. She's so sweet."

"I can't wait to see you too, Gram but you better not be trying to set me up. You know I won't date anyone at your assisted living facility."

"You worry too much. I won't be here forever."

"Gram," I warn, my heart clenching. Losing her is not something I want to talk about, ever.

With a heavy sigh, she changes the subject, "Fine. What time will you be here? I can meet you down in the kitchen."

"I'll be there at noon, but I'm bringing you lunch this time. Don't even think about making anything."

She laughs. "Got it. You sound just like your father."

I cringe, swiftly shaking it off, knowing she means it as a compliment. "Gram, I gotta go. I need to be at the site early."

"Alright. Have a good day, Kelly. I love you."

"Thanks, Gram. I love you too."

Disconnecting, I slip my phone in my pocket, striding towards the kitchen. My eyes go wide and my mouth goes dry at the sight of Sloane bent over, searching through a cabinet with her ass in the air, barely covered by frilly white shorts. The view gives me all kinds of ideas of how and where I want to take her from behind making my heart race and my dick hard. I clench my fists taking a deep breath hoping to calm my dirty thoughts to no avail.

"Good morning," I moan, grinning wide as she spins to face me. My eyes drift down her body, her fitted pale blue, long-sleeved shirt holding tight to her full breasts. Damn.

"What are you doing here?" she asks making me chuckle.

"I live here. Did you forget already?"

She huffs, glaring at me. Spinning on her heel, she grabs a black coffee mug out of the cabinet, filling it with fresh coffee. "No, I meant–just forget it."

"Done."

Pinching her lips tightly together, she leans back, resting against the counter. Cupping the mug of hot coffee, she closes her eyes, inhaling deeply. Her tongue juts out, licking her lips, my eyes glued to every movement. Desperate for a taste, I step into her space, her eyes fly open, meeting my gaze. A soft gasp escapes her lips. Her breathing picks up, my dick twitching. Reaching above her head, I pull out my red Christmas mug painted with a white beard and mustache, settling for pouring myself a cup of coffee before stepping back.

She straightens, taking another sip. "I, um... I have to work today, so is there anything I can do for you before I leave?"

The corners of my lips curve up in a salacious grin. "There's a lot you could do for me if you're willing."

Flushing instantly, she stammers, "No, that's not... not like...I didn't mean... You... Ugh!"

Laughing, I let her off the hook–sort of. "Get your mind out of the gutter, Pixie. There's dishes, cleaning my room, laundry. I'm sure you could come up with something."

"I'm not doing that."

"Got it. I'll be gone for a while anyway." Letting my gaze drift over her one more time, I take a sip of my coffee, forcing myself to walk away before I get myself into trouble; well, more than I already did. "Have a good day, Pixie."

Just before I step back into my room, she calls out, "Why do you keep calling me that? My name is Sloane."

Nodding, I insist, "Oh, I know, Sloane, but Pixie is so fitting I can't seem to help myself."

"Why do you say that?"

"Maybe if you're good, you'll find out." I wink, watching her blush a deep, beautiful shade of red. Clenching my jaw, I force myself to walk away for a second time. "See you later, Pixie."

"Damn that man," she mumbles under her breath, not realizing I could hear making me chuckle.

The rest of my morning flies by with everything at the construction site seeming to be on track. Thankfully, it helps so I'm able to get out of there for lunch. Smiling across the table at my grandmother, I relax back in my seat. She grins cheekily, handing me a plate of cookies. "You said you wouldn't make anything."

"No, you said you were bringing lunch and asked me not to make any, but you didn't say a thing about dessert," she retorts, arching her eyebrows in challenge. I laugh.

"Gram–"

"Kelly," she interrupts, sitting a little straighter. "I wanted to introduce you to one of my nurses. She's such a sweetheart."

"Gram, I told you, you're not setting me up with anyone here."

"Are you seeing someone?"

"No. I just moved here and I'm not looking to get into a relationship right now, Gram."

She brightens, her eyes dancing, despite my comment. The moment she opens her mouth, I know why. "That's right. You just moved in with Sloane Douglas. She's such a sweet girl. Well, I suppose she's not a girl anymore, but you know what I mean."

Yeah, she's right there. Everything about her so far tells me she's all woman. "Gram, nothing is happening between Sloane and me. I'm her roommate. That's it."

She waves me away as if I'm being ridiculous. "She's a sweet woman. It was so nice of her to offer you her spare room. You know, I want to do something nice for her to thank her for renting to you."

"You don't have to do that."

"Well, it's kind of something for you too. I had Ralph get down the Christmas boxes from the hall closet this morning so you and I could decorate and there's so much more than I would be able to use here."

I shake my head. "Gram, I can't take your things."

"I'll have plenty. In fact, why don't you help me finish decorating and then you take everything we don't use here to decorate your new place. Besides, I have things I want you to have like ornaments and other decorations that were always meant for you. And I'm sure Sloane would love it too."

Sloane's rules flash in my mind, but she had to be talking about changing the style of the apartment, not this kind of decorating. Right? Everybody loves Christmas and I'm not about to wipe my grandmother's hopeful expression off her face. "That sounds good, Gram. I'm sure Sloane would love that as much as I will. You know I appreciate everything you do for me."

Smiling brightly, she holds out her hand, reaching towards me, urging, "Come here, Kelly." I do as she says. Grabbing her hand, I crouch down in front of her. Gently, she pats my cheek. "You deserve all the good things, my boy. I think this will be your Christmas."

My heart clenches. She says that every year. I couldn't ask for a better grandmother. Leaning towards her, I wrap my arms around her, giving her a gentle hug, careful not to squeeze too tight. "I love you, Gram."

"I love you too, Kelly." I stand up, always happy to help her. She smiles, happiness shining in her eyes. "Now, let's get to work. The boxes are over there," she directs, pointing.

Pushing up my sleeves, I stride towards the boxes full of everything Christmas.

Chapter 4

Sloane

My feet are killing me. The flower and garden center was packed today. Everyone is busy buying poinsettias and amaryllis for holiday parties or sending any mix of Christmas colored flowers; carnations and roses the most popular. It's usually not this busy, but today felt like there was something big going on. My lunch break was spent taking care of the greenhouse. Yet, I still had to stay late to finish.

The only thing I want to do now, is collapse on the couch, order food, and watch TV.

Sighing heavily, I park my car in the driveway and suck my bottom lip between my teeth. I wonder if Kelly will be home. Honestly, I wonder if he's going to keep giving me a hard time. It doesn't matter that I see what he's doing, he gets me so flustered I can't even call him on it.

Groaning, I climb out of my car, trudging to the front door, my nerves swirling in the pit of my stomach. I shouldn't be this nervous to come home. I'm living with him. It's time to start getting used to it.

Taking a deep breath, I push the door open, keeping my focus on doing the simple tasks, one foot in front of the other. Slipping off my coat, I hang it up with my purse on the hooks behind the door.

"Hey, Pixie. Have a good day?" His gravelly voice rolls over my skin eliciting goose bumps.

Forcing a smile, I turn on my heel and face Kelly, gasping at the sight of my living room. Kelly stands in the middle of open boxes scattered around the room with Christmas decorations sticking out of the top of every single one. Instantly flooded with memories, my chest tightens. I fight to keep my emotions at bay. "What the hell is all this? I thought you moved in yesterday."

A sexy smirk curves his lips as he nods. "I did. My Gram gave me some Christmas decorations. She thought we would both like them and since you don't have any up yet, I thought I'd take a look and see what she sent over."

Shaking my head in disbelief, I bring my gaze back to him. "You can't put that up in here."

His eyebrows draw down in confusion. "What?"

"Did you forget the rules already?"

He huffs a laugh. "No, but I thought you were talking about things like furniture, pictures, vases, and those figurines women like or something. I didn't think you meant Christmas decorations."

Crossing my arms over my chest, I narrow my eyes, insisting, "I definitely meant Christmas decorations."

He clenches his jaw, his hands falling to his hips as he stares at me, getting his obvious frustration with me under control. "I'm sorry, Pixie. My mistake. Do you not celebrate Christmas?"

"No, I do, but..." I shake my head, my stomach twisting at the thought of explaining my life to him. At my age, it shouldn't matter anymore what kind of family dynamic I have, but sometimes it hits me hard. That's when I struggle to move past it. Every single year, Christmas is one of those times. In my own home, I ignore it. Hell, I don't deal with it at all until I absolutely have to. It works for me. "Can't you just follow one simple rule?"

"Sure, if it makes sense."

"What's that supposed to mean?"

He takes a step towards me, holding his arms up as if he's trying to calm a caged animal. "It just means, I shouldn't have to give up my beliefs and traditions without a reason."

He's right, but it's been such a long day that this feels like a slap in the face. "Fine. You can do whatever you want in your bedroom, but not in here. Is that too much to ask?"

"You know my bed takes up most of my room. Well, of course you don't because you haven't seen it...yet."

"Ugh!" I blush, storming towards the kitchen, needing to move before I break down or hit him. Besides, I'm hungry.

The moment I turn the corner, my footsteps falter and I halt, looking around the room. Dishes are piled high in the sink, a trail of something goes from the sink to the stove and used frying pans still sit on the burner. "What happened in here?"

His heated breath on the back of my neck startles me, sending a shiver down my spine. "Yeah, sorry about that. I'm going to clean that up, but I'm one man and I also have all the other boxes. I'll get it done."

"How am I supposed to...just forget it." I shake my head and push past him, ignoring the electricity shooting up my arm at his touch. Making my way towards the bathroom, I slip inside and shut the door behind me.

Maybe it wouldn't have been so bad to move home. Who am I kidding? It would've been worse than this. Besides, Kelly already made my dreams more interesting after only one night. I just won't be admitting that to him. Sighing, I slip my pants down and sit, losing my balance as I sink deeper than expected, my ass hitting the cold water making me scream. "Ah!"

A knock immediately sounds at the door. "Sloane, are you okay?"

The handle jiggles and my eyes widen in panic. Shoving myself out of the toilet, I launch myself at the door, tripping over my pants, halfway down my legs. "Don't come in!" I yell, slurring as if it's one word. My hip clips the corner of the sink, and I crash to the floor with a thud, missing the door completely. "Shit."

"Fuck," he mumbles under his breath, standing over me as my skin heats to the color of a tomato.

I meet his gaze for just a moment before he crouches down by my head, keeping his eyes on mine. "You all right, Pixie?" he asks, his voice low and tender.

With tears in my eyes and pinpricks in my throat, I beg, "I'm fine, just get out, please."

Pressing his lips together, he nods. Veering his gaze away from me, he slips out the door. Defeated, I sigh heavily and pick myself up off the floor, finishing up. After cleaning myself up and washing my hands, I splash my face with cold water. Heaving a sigh, I step out the bathroom door and into my bedroom.

The moment my door closes, I lean against it and slide to the floor, my tears breaking free. I'm such a klutz! Of course, I'm the one who has to get rescued by that man, even if it was his fault it happened at all. Apparently, I can only make a fool of myself in front of him.

And of course, it comes right after I yell at him for all of his Christmas decorations. I hate that something so simple still crushes me. The moment I see a Santa hat, I can't think straight, or I guess, do anything at all. It's ridiculous. Christmas should be a happy time of year, but my head goes into emotional chaos throwing me so out of whack that I can't manage basics. I can only imagine what Kelly thinks of me. My stomach twists into knots at the thought.

A soft knock vibrates my back, but I remain silent, wiping my tears. "Pixie," he calls softly. Another knock. "Pixie, you okay?"

"I'm fine," I retort, knowing I'm the opposite of okay, but how do I confess my story to the hot stranger now living with me that likely just got an eyeful?

"Okay," he mumbles dragging out the word. "Listen, I didn't see anything, well not for long."

"Ugh," I groan, banging my head against the door.

"I just mean I looked away as soon as I realized."

"Doesn't help."

"When I see that part of you, Pixie, it'll be because you want to share it with me, not because I forgot to put the seat down."

"Gee, thanks."

He sighs heavily, pausing. "I'm sorry, Sloane. I know that was my fault. And after that, for the first time in my life I can say with complete confidence that I don't think I'll ever forget to put the seat down again."

I huff a laugh, quickly covering my mouth.

"Ah, I heard that. You're smiling. I'll take it." I suck my lip between my teeth, remaining silent. "Okay, I concede. I'll lay off the Christmas decorations, for now, but we'll talk about that later. In the meantime, I ordered a pizza. It should be here in a few minutes if you're hungry."

His footsteps retreat before I register his words. He's waving the white flag, giving me a peace offering. I smile, knowing it's time to seize it.

Taking a deep breath, I push myself off the floor and try to pull myself together. I grab a pair of gray leggings and a navy blue, off the shoulder sweatshirt, along with a clean bra and underwear. Slipping back into the bathroom, I attempt to clean off the day and scrub off my embarrassment.

Too bad it's not that simple.

Chapter 5

Kelly

With a large pizza in hand, I glance at the table full of Christmas boxes and walk over to the coffee table instead, setting it down. Pausing, I readjust myself again, thoughts of Sloane laying on the bathroom floor pushing themselves to the forefront of my mind. It may have only been a brief accidental moment, but it only confirmed what I already knew. I want her bad.

Making my way towards the kitchen, I grab a couple glasses and some water, wondering what she likes. The simple thought instantly turning dirty. Fuck. I have to pull my head away from my dick.

Remembering the look on her face the moment I met her gaze does the trick. She looked so vulnerable; defeated. It broke my fucking heart. The least I can do is end our undeclared war no matter how much fun I'm having teasing her. After all, it's my damn fault that happened. I guess after living with my mom and dad for so long, everything they taught me slips away the moment I break free from them. Sure, I'm determined to be nothing like them, but that doesn't mean I have to make Sloane miserable in the process.

Before I walk out of the kitchen, I swipe some paper towels to use in place of napkins and stick those under my arm, carrying them along with two glasses of water. Hopefully, she'll come and eat.

The moment I sit on the couch, setting everything down, the bathroom door opens and Sloane steps into the hallway. Freshly showered, she looks more gorgeous than ever with an off the shoulder pale pink sweatshirt and her long hair pulled up in a messy bun on top of her head making me want to press my face into her neck and nibble, inhaling her scent.

Pulling my thoughts back to the present, I notice her stiff movements as she approaches, likely uncomfortable from earlier. "Hungry?" I ask, attempting to ignore the elephant in the room.

She breathes a sigh of relief, her body sagging as she sits near me on the couch to reach the pizza. "Starving."

"It's sausage, green peppers, and tomatoes."

"Sounds good. I eat almost anything except onions and anchovies."

I quirk a brow, "Pineapple?"

"On the right pizza, sure."

"You're a brave soul." I smirk, handing her a slice on a paper plate. "I have enough dishes to do already."

She giggles, settling into the couch, the light sound running over my skin. "Yes, you do." I watch as she takes a bite of the pizza, a soft moan of pleasure escaping as she chews.

Taking a deep breath, I swiftly attempt to redirect my thoughts. "So, why do you hate Christmas?"

Huffing a laugh, she coughs. Leaning forward, she sets the pizza down and takes a drink of water. Bashfully, glancing up at me from underneath her long lashes. "I hope that was for me?" I nod. She clears her throat, taking another drink. "Thank you." Heaving a sigh, she claims, "I don't hate Christmas." I arch my eyebrows and pinch my lips together, hoping she'll elaborate in the silence. "Well, it just brings back some bad memories for me."

Her admission squeezes my heart. "Ah. Now that I understand," I concede, taking a bite of pizza.

"You don't get along with your family?" she asks, attempting to turn this back on me.

My lips twitch. "We weren't talking about me."

"We are now." She grins, eliciting a chuckle.

"Okay, fine. We'll compromise. You share something about you and I'll do the same."

Hesitating, she sucks her bottom lip between her teeth, drawing my attention. I lick my lips, tracking her movement. My mouth salivates, desperate to get a taste of her. "Fine. But we take turns going first and asking a question."

Cocking my head to the side, I taunt, "Do we need to shake or kiss on it?"

"Nah, I'm good." Her lips twitch.

"I'm sure you are." She opens her mouth to retort, but I don't give her the chance, asking, "What kind of bad memories do you have of Christmas?"

Flinching, she requests, "Can we start with something easier?"

"Sure," I concede, nodding, my thoughts drifting to the first time we met. My lips tug up, my eyes shining with mischief. "Are your panties pink like your vibrator?"

She gasps, flushing, giving me my desired effect. Then she straightens and surprisingly answers. "Some of them, yes, it's my favorite color, but I have a rainbow of panties to choose from."

My mouth falls open, my breath becoming ragged. Damn, what did I just get myself into? "Um..."

"And no, you still can't see them." She winks, making me laugh. "All right, my turn."

"Go ahead, you've earned it."

"You don't get along with your family?"

My eyes narrow. "I thought we were starting easy."

"For me."

I laugh. "Oh, I see how it is." Pausing, I take another bite of my pizza, trying to come up with how to word it without looking like an asshole. I swallow and look her in the eyes. "My parents are part of their own little world with rules that I don't like to abide by, but they expect me to anyway."

"I've already seen how much you don't like rules."

Huffing a laugh, I nod. "Yeah, but their rules are attached to my parents love and approval. I'm a grown ass man. I don't need that type of judgement."

She sucks her bottom lip into her mouth once again, running her teeth over it before releasing it. "I get it. That's kinda the same reason I needed you to move in, so I didn't have to move back home."

"The flower and garden business isn't doing well?"

She shrugs. "It is, but it's not my business."

"Ah. And what is it you want to do, Pixie?"

She grins, her eyes warming as she answers. "I'd love to do more landscape design. I have a degree in landscape architecture. It's so much fun to help create an outdoor space. You know?" She shrugs like it's no big deal. "Well, sometimes it's an indoor garden space, but... Either way, there's not a lot of interest for something like that in a small coastal town like this."

"There may be more than you think."

"What do you mean?"

"What about the remodel on the Sagerton property? I heard they were looking for someone just like you."

Her eyebrows draw down. "How do you know about that? Are you working on that project?"

I open my mouth to respond when there's a knock at the door. She looks at me, narrowing her eyes and I hold my hands up in defense. "I didn't invite anyone over."

She sets her nearly empty plate down and stands. "Coming." I sit back, my eyes drawn to her ass as she walks towards the door. Pushing up on her tiptoes, she peeks through the peephole and instantly falls back on her heels with a huff. Yanking the door open, she crosses her arms over her chest, pushing up her cleavage and glares at the person on the other side. "What the hell are you doing here?"

A man with dark, perfectly combed hair stands in the doorway, shifting from one foot to the other, his eyes widening the moment he sees Sloane, an irrational wave of jealousy instantly washing over me.

Chapter 6

Sloane

"What the hell are you doing here?" I ask, glaring up at Dan.

"I'm here to see you, Sloane. I was hoping we could talk."

"Don't you know how to use a phone? You should've called."

"True, but I didn't think you'd answer."

"You're right."

He steps into my space. My body stiffens, but I refuse to back away. "Come on, Sloane. Let me in. I just want to talk. I miss you."

"No, you don't. You're just lonely with Fiona out of town."

His face falls as if I'm the one who damaged us. "That's not fair."

"I'll tell you what's fair," I begin just as a warm body comes up behind me, his large hands falling to my shoulders and giving them a gentle squeeze causing my heart to skip a beat.

"All good, Pixie?"

"Ah, yeah," I mumble, unmoving.

"Pixie?" Dan retorts, arching his eyebrows.

"It's my nickname for my woman," Kelly declares grinning as he wraps one arm around me, pulling my back flush to his front, my body heating instantly.

Dan arches his eyebrows. "Your woman?"

Instead of answering, he reaches out with his other hand, introducing himself. "Kelly Travers. And you are?"

Dan glances at his hand, grinding his jaw before he takes it, reluctantly shaking it. "Sloane's–"

"You're not my anything," I interrupt.

They both glance at me before breaking their handshake. "This was obviously a bad time. I'll come by when you don't have...company." He frowns.

My body vibrates as Kelly chuckles. "Good luck with that since I live here."

Dan's mouth drops open. "You live with this asshole."

Finally getting my footing, I step away from Kelly, placing my hand on his chest and pushing him back, my fingers tingling at the contact. "Go. I've got this."

He looks down at me and nods, giving Dan one last glance. "Okay."

My gaze veers to Dan. He points at Kelly. "Sloane–"

"Don't bother Dan. You have no right. What about Fiona?" He opens his mouth to answer, but I hold my hand up, stopping him. "It doesn't matter. Just go."

"Wait, Sloane. I came over to tell you that we'll be at your dad's place for Christmas."

"Of course, you will. Please, just go, Dan."

"I'll see you later," he mutters as I shut the door in his face and walk back towards Kelly sitting on the couch.

"That was the ex-boyfriend, huh?"

I grimace. "Ex-fiancé."

"Ouch. What happened?"

"We broke up. What was with the posturing?"

"Looked like you needed help."

I scoff. "I can handle him just fine."

"Doesn't mean you should have to." He scrunches his nose up and asks, "You dated that asshole?"

Heaving a sigh, I admit, "Yeah, I know. But he wasn't like that when I was dating him."

"You mean he wasn't like that around you when you were dating him."

"Probably." I shrug, conceding.

"Why is he going to be at your dad's place for Christmas?"

I make a face. "Because he's dating my stepmom's daughter."

His eyes widen. "That sucks."

"You're not kidding. I can't believe I have to spend any part of Christmas with them."

"Is that why you hate Christmas so much?"

"Part of it, but I don't exactly hate Christmas."

He arches his eyebrows in challenge. "You sure about that?"

"I'm sure. It's the memories it's connected to," I admit surprising myself, but I guess seeing Dan was the door to allowing everything to spill out.

"What kind of memories?" he asks, his voice full of empathy.

"The kind of memories that crush a child." Pausing, I take a deep breath, revealing, "My dad left days before Christmas when I was a kid. That year my brother and I had to fend for ourselves while our mother spent the rest of the month crying in her room. We ate dry cereal for dinner and there were no presents under the tree. I wrapped a toy from my room with my blanket and gave it to my brother so he would have something. Obviously, he knew, but..."

He reaches out grabbing my hand, giving it a squeeze, shooting tingles straight up my arm. "I'm sorry you had to deal with all that. You're a good sister."

My lips curl up. "Thanks." His thumb runs over the back of my hand in comfort and I take a moment, relishing the feeling. Clearing my throat, I continue, "Anyway, my dad has dated a few women, but he married Fiona's mom a couple years ago, I guess. In fact, Dan met Fiona at their wedding because he was there with me."

"You think he was cheating on you?"

"Not the whole time, but yeah, I do."

"Sounds like they're both assholes."

I huff a laugh. "True. Anyway, I just gave you almost everything without you sharing a word."

He smirks. "I wasn't about to stop you." Pausing, he stares at me, holding my gaze. My heart begins to race, while I get lost in his eyes. "Are you bringing anyone to your family Christmas?"

"Ah, no. I've only ever brought a boyfriend, or I guess a fiancé and I don't have one of those at the moment."

Tilting his head to the side he asks, "What if I went with you?"

My eyes widen and my mouth falls open. "What? Why would you want to go to my dad's for Christmas?"

"Hear me out. Douch-bag already thinks I'm your live-in boyfriend. Wouldn't it be strange if I didn't come? And it would probably be tolerable dealing with him if you have a buffer."

My eyes narrow, waiting for the other side of this deal I know is coming. "If you go to my dad's, you'd have to go to my mom's. She'd expect it."

"No problem." He grins wide.

"Again, why would you want to?"

Releasing my hand, he leans back, his arm falling to the back of the couch. "The Saturday night before Christmas, my parents have a big Christmas party that I'd rather not go to, but I have no choice. I spend most of my time fending off women or setups I don't want. I'd only ask that you come with me to that party as my date."

My stomach turns and I suck my lower lip between my teeth. I've read about something like this in my romance novels, but never in real life. In books though, they always end up together and I know that won't happen. Kelly is too much of a player.

Releasing my lip, I clarify, "I usually go to my mom's on Christmas morning and my dad's for Christmas dinner. That's your whole Christmas."

He shrugs, giving me a crooked smile. "Fine by me. And we still have Christmas Eve."

We. I arch my eyebrows in question and suck my lower lip between my teeth once again in thought. His eyes flare, licking his lips as he watches me shooting heat straight to my core. "Um...you ah...you don't have other plans for Christmas? Or, um, Christmas Eve?"

Shaking his head, his eyes soften as he admits, "I'll want to spend some time on either day with my grandmother. She's just up the road at the assisted living facility. I'm sure we have plenty of time."

I gasp. There's that word again–we. "Your grandmother? Is that why you moved here?"

"Yeah. My parents are alive, but she's my family, well, her and my uncle, but he's my mom's side of the family."

My chest tightens, making it difficult to breathe as I stare at Kelly, realizing he's so much more than I'm giving him credit for. "I'm sorry."

"I'm not."

Nodding, I pull my lower lip into my mouth, running my teeth over it again, wondering if spending Christmas with Kelly as my fake boyfriend is a good idea. Knowing I'm incredibly attracted to him and I'm a relationship kind of woman, probably not, but I don't know if I care. It would take away so much pressure and the looks of pity everyone would give me. Instead, I could walk in with a sexy man like Kelly.

But what if it doesn't go well and we still have to live in the same space? Then again, that would only put me right back where I started.

"You're thinking too much. I see it." Kelly inches closer, my heartbeat picking up its pace, my eyes drawn to his every move. Reaching towards me, he runs his thumb over my upper lip, his touch electric. "Every time that lip disappears into your mouth, I want to kiss you and suck it into mine," he reveals, his voice coming out raspy, igniting me from the inside out.

My body tingles in anticipation. Whimpering, I lean towards him. In seconds, he meets me halfway, pressing his soft lips to mine. My hands wrap around his neck and his fingers weave into my hair as he cradles my face in his hands. Tilting his head, he gently sucks my lips towards him until our tongues collide in a frantic kiss. Licking, tasting, exploring. He deepens the kiss, and I happily become a willing participant.

Straddling his lap, I sit back, our mouths never parting, continuing their dance. My nipples go taut, straining to reach him, my core heating, swelling, craving his touch.

Suddenly, a cell phone rings pulling me out of the moment. I tear my lips away from his, both of us gasping for breath as we let reality set in.

Scrambling out of his lap, I stumble. He grasps my arms, so I don't fall. Swiftly, I get my feet under me and ramble, "Um, I ah, that's you. I mean your phone. And um, I ah, I have to use the, um, bathroom. Yup. You should answer that." Spinning on my heel, I all but sprint for the bathroom, knowing I have nowhere to escape.

I shut the door behind me, splashing my face with cold water. Leaning on the sink I look into the mirror, mumbling to myself, "This is such a good, but also very bad idea."

Chapter 7

Kelly

That kiss. Fuck, it was hot. I want more, but does she? I'd be a happy man if Sloane was all I got for Christmas, but I don't think she's ready. The way she looks at me, I know I'm not the only one feeling this fire between us, but I see her going into her head thinking too much. It makes me question if she wants this at all.

My cell phone stops ringing and immediately starts ringing again. I glance at the screen, my mother's name flashing. Grimacing, I ignore it, but the ringing continues. With a heavy sigh, I swipe my phone off the table and answer.

Before I get a word in, my mom blurts out, "Why haven't you answered any of my calls or texts, Kelly?"

"Hi, Mom."

"Are you too busy to answer a simple question?"

Heaving a sigh, I run my hand down my face and over the scruff of my jaw. "What question is that?" I ask, already knowing the answer.

"You know the Christmas party is in less than two weeks, and I expect you to be there."

"Is there a question in there?" I ask, knowing I'm pushing the boundaries.

"Kelly James Travers, you know what I'm asking."

"Sure, Mom. I'll be there."

"Good. I have someone I want to introduce you to."

And so, it begins. I hope like hell Sloane is on board with this because I'm off and running. "That's great as long as it's not a set up. My girlfriend wouldn't take too kindly to you trying to set me up."

"Girlfriend?" she shrieks making me flinch. "You have a girlfriend and you didn't even tell your own mother?"

Like you give a damn. "Yeah, I have a girlfriend, Mom and she's coming with me to the Christmas party. I didn't tell you about her because I thought I was too old for that shit, and you didn't ask."

"Kelly, watch your mouth. You–"

I interrupt, "Look, Mom, I gotta go."

"Wait! What's her name?"

"Sloane," I answer and disconnect before she has a chance to ask any other questions. Tossing my phone on the coffee table, I groan and flop back against the couch cushions.

"Who were you talking to?" Sloane asks, startling me.

"Pixie. I didn't see you walk back in the room."

"I heard my name," she continues.

Nodding, I admit, "Yeah, that was my mom. I hope you're in this with me because I just lied to my mom and told her my girlfriend was coming with me to our Christmas party. She was already planning who to set me up with."

She nods, sucking that damn lip between her teeth once again. "Okay," she mumbles, dragging out the word. "If we're going to do this, we probably need to spend some more time getting to know each other."

"So, that means you're not backing out?"

"No. I can't believe I'm saying this, but we're in this together. How about we clean up dinner and look through your boxes?"

The corners of my lips curve up. "Hold up. Are you saying we can actually decorate this place for Christmas?"

"Yes, that's exactly what I'm saying. I think it's time. I'll even turn on the Christmas music to get us in the mood."

Smirking, I wiggle my eyebrows. "Sounds good to me."

She giggles shaking her head in amusement. "So, what do you have in these boxes anyway?"

"I just started looking through them when you walked in earlier, so I don't really know."

"Maybe we should find out." She dances across the room, appearing almost giddy bringing a smile to my face. That's a big one-eighty for someone who didn't like Christmas a few minutes ago and I don't want to see it slip away.

Ripping the tape off an opened box, I lift the flaps and peer inside. Two six-inch elves stand with their arms around one another smiling. Picking it up, I flip it over, checking for batteries. "What's that?" Sloane asks.

"When it's working, the elves sway back and forth singing *Happy Xmas*, you know, *The War is Over* song?"

"That's cute."

"When I was really little, the closer it got to Christmas, the harder it was for me to go to sleep. My gram used to play this and it would be the only thing that would keep me in bed. I don't know why."

"It's a good song."

"Yeah, but it was more than that for me. Maybe it was more like what I wished for with my family." I shake my head, shocked at my admission and try to move on. "You know what anyone would want as a kid."

Out of the corner of my eye, Sloane gives me a look I can't quite decipher. Stepping around the table, I attempt to refocus. "So, is it just you and your brother?"

Swiftly clearing her throat, she begins pulling things out of the first box and setting them on the table. "Yeah, Jake is two years older than me."

"Older? By the way you were talking I thought you were older."

"No, but I guess you could say we take care of each other."

My chest tightens, not ever really knowing what that was like–having a sibling I could depend on, no questions asked. "I like that."

"Me too. What about you? Any brothers or sisters?"

Shaking my head, I admit, "Only child, but lots of cousins." I pull out ornaments one by one and set them on the table. "Looks like we might need a Christmas tree to put some of these on."

"Yeah, I guess."

"You know, people talk in small towns," I emphasize, an idea forming in my head.

"They do." She nods.

"So, to get people to believe we're dating, we should probably be seen in public together before Christmas. Maybe we can pick out a Christmas tree this weekend," I suggest, watching her close to see her reaction.

She glances up at me but doesn't respond as she reaches across the table and pulls out an ornament. I'm not sure if that's her answer or not. "These have dates on the bottom. Are they all like that?"

"Probably. My grandmother is very sentimental," I divulge and she smiles, her beauty momentarily taking my breath.

Tearing my gaze away, I look down at the round glass ornament in my hand, my eyes narrowing at a large black polka-dot shuffling towards my thumb. Gasping, I jump, spinning around and throwing it hard, flinching as it shatters against the wall into thousands of pieces. "Shit."

"What's wrong?" Sloane asks, her eyes going wide.

Frowning, I give a shake of my head. "Nothing."

Crossing her arms over her chest, she looks at me, arching her eyebrows and calling me on my bullshit. "You threw an ornament against the wall like you were pitching a fastball and shattered it. That wasn't nothing."

Clenching my jaw, I exhale harshly, hating that she caught a weakness, but I don't lie. "Fine. There was a spider on it."

"What?" she asks, huffing a laugh. Great.

"There was a huge furry spider on the ornament crawling for my hand. Happy now?"

Her head falls back in laughter, the sight stunning. "A spider?" she questions, barely able to speak through her giggles.

"Yes, a spider. I hate them, okay?"

She laughs harder at my expense, collapsing onto the couch as she tries to catch her breath. "Never would've thought with all that muscle you would be afraid of a little old spider."

"You noticed my muscles?" I tease, but she keeps laughing. "It wasn't little." Pointing towards the ground, I insist, "Look, there it is!"

A black spider scampers swiftly across the floor, my finger following its every move causing another burst of laughter to erupt from her chest. "That's not furry. You made me think it was the size of a mouse."

My eyes narrow, glaring at her. "Will you just get rid of it?" She stares at me grinning like a Cheshire cat. "Please."

"Okay." I watch as she stands, swiping her cup of water and downing it before grabbing a piece of paper off the coffee table. She saunters towards the spider, catching it before stepping towards me with a proud smile. "I got it."

"I don't want to see it!"

Shrugging, she smirks. "Fine, but maybe I'll put it in your bed to find later." She takes a step towards my bedroom prompting me to react. Moving suddenly, I'm barely thinking as I step up right behind her.

"Sloane! Don't even think about it or I'll be sleeping in your bed."

Her body flushes instantly and my dick twitches. Keeping my focus on her, I watch as she takes a deep breath, before striding towards the window, yanking it open and shaking the spider out of the cup. I hope. "Fine."

"Why didn't you just kill it? It will freeze anyway. It's cold tonight."

"It's not that cold, we live in North Carolina." I give her a look and she scrunches her nose up adorably. "I should've put it down your shirt. It's the least you deserve after making Christmas throw up in my apartment."

Chuckling, I claim, "We've barely gotten started on decorating and you're lucky you didn't get it anywhere near me."

"And what would've happened if I did?" she asks, her eyes flashing with a fire that fans my flames.

"Care to find out?"

She sucks in her bottom lip, and I lick mine in response, wanting another taste. Living with her just might be pure torture. "Maybe, but for now, we have some more decorating to do."

I smirk. "I'll clean up the glass first but go ahead and keep going through my stuff." The smile she rewards me with makes my chest tight and is so damn worth it.

Chapter 8

Sloane

"Okay, let me get this straight," Alex's voice echoes through my phone, "last night you kissed him, and you put up Christmas decorations together? Damn, this is getting serious."

"Alex, I'm being serious."

"So am I, Sloane. Christmas decorations," she emphasizes.

Groaning, I add, "You're right. I know. And now he wants to go pick out a Christmas tree together."

"Well, you're already in deep with the decorations, what's so bad about Christmas tree shopping?"

"Nothing except he doesn't really want to date me. He wants to be my fake boyfriend and pretend to go on dates."

"I didn't see anything fake about the way he was eye fucking you at the bar," she interrupts.

"Gee, thanks. But I can't do a one-night stand or whatever this is. You know I'm insanely attracted to him, and I already see a soft side to him. You know I'm a sucker for a sweet side."

"So, what are you trying to say, Sloane? You're screwed?"

"I'm saying that if I go through with this fake dating thing, I'm going to fall for him and he's going to leave me high and dry after he has his way with me."

"As long as he has his way with you first because I'm sure the sex would be fantastic."

"Alex..."

"I'm not wrong." I huff and she laughs. "Okay, okay. So, you already know he doesn't want to be in a relationship?"

"Not exactly, but you saw him at the bar. He's a big flirt. And he wants to take me to his family Christmas party as a buffer, so he doesn't get set up or asked out by women looking for a committed relationship."

"But you didn't ask him if he wants a girlfriend? Or at least if he's against having one?"

"No, but..."

"Don't ever assume. Give the guy–" A loud noise followed by yelling sounds in the background. "I'm sorry, Sloane, but I have to go."

"Everything okay?"

"Yeah, fine. Bye, Sloane." Alex disconnects before I get another word in, leaving me staring at the screen.

With a sigh, I slip my phone in my pocket and wander towards the kitchen, my stomach growling. The moment I step into the hall, the smell of a sweet and savory marinara sauce hits my senses. "Mm, that smells good," I mumble stepping into the kitchen.

"Thanks," Kelly answers, maintaining his position at the stove with his back to me dressed in faded blue jeans, a thin, navy blue fitted Henley and bare feet. The sight of him looking sexy and all domestic in my kitchen makes my mouth water. "I made spaghetti and meatballs, along with garlic bread and a Caesar salad. It's nothing fancy, but there's more than enough for both of us if you're hungry."

"Thank you. I would love some. I was just coming out here to figure out what to make for dinner."

He glances over his shoulder, giving me a heart melting smile causing mine to flutter. "Well, I guess it's good I was hoping you would agree to join me then."

My face heats at the same time goose bumps erupt over my skin. Quickly, I avert my gaze. "Is there anything I can do to help?"

"You can bring the salad and garlic bread to the table and grab us something to drink."

Nodding, I get to work. Having a man in my kitchen never felt more natural than it does in this moment, but I'm not letting my imagination run wild. At least not before I get to know him better, and maybe not even then...

A few minutes later, I'm sitting across from Kelly taking my first bite of spaghetti. "Mm. This is delicious. Thank you."

"You're welcome. I figured it's the least I could do."

"Why do you say that? You don't owe me anything."

"Yeah, I do. For the Christmas decorations, for sharing, for listening, for letting me stay."

"Kelly..."

Interrupting, he continues, "And for coming with me to the Christmas party. That's huge for me. You have no idea."

"I'd love to understand. You said it's your family Christmas party. What could be so awful that you want little me to protect you?" I joke, attempting to keep the conversation light.

He meets my gaze, the light in his eyes diminishing when he nods squeezing my heart. "Ask me anything."

"You said it was family, but it's obviously more than family if your mom is trying to set you up with women there."

His head falls back in laughter. "That's not a question, Pixie. You're right, but that's not even close to a question."

"Sorry."

"Don't be. I assume you want to know why?"

Shrugging, I concede, "Well, yeah. Usually, Christmas is about family. Why would your mom continue to try to set you up if that's not what you want? As you pointed out, you're a grown-ass man." I smirk.

He swallows hard, pushing food around on his plate as he talks. "This Christmas party is more about business, how my parents want to portray themselves with their friends and in the community and honestly showing off. My parents have a certain ideal they set for me long before I was born and let's just say I haven't lived up to their expectations. Sometimes I feel like I'm more of a trophy for them to wave around."

"That's bullshit."

He huffs a laugh. "That's putting it mildly, but I'm old enough that I've dealt with it. They keep trying to set me up with women they think I should be dating, but I always find a way out. Christmas is the one time I can't find an excuse to stay away because they would rather have me at this party than have me spend time with them on Christmas." His lips twitch. "But this year I don't have to worry because I have you."

"You have me?" I quirk a brow, sucking my lower lip into my mouth.

Leaning forward, he moans. "You keep doing that, I sure as hell will."

My head falls back as I burst out laughing. "You're pretty confident there, aren't you?"

"I did already get you to agree to let me live with you and be my girlfriend for Christmas."

Sighing, I shake my head. "And yet I feel like there's still so much I don't know about you, Kelly, except you're a huge flirt."

"Is that what you think?"

"That's what I know. Don't you remember the night we met?"

Licking his lips, he gives me a crooked grin. "I won't ever forget. Pink panties and vibrators, yet you still haven't shared. How is that fair?"

"Kelly," I warn, flushing, but I'm not quite sure what I'm warning him about.

"Besides, you know a lot more about me than that, Pixie. I know I sure haven't forgotten that kiss. Do I need to remind you?"

My body ignites and my heartbeat picks up its pace at the memory. "No, nope. I remember."

"You know you're going to have to be comfortable with me in public. I'm an affectionate man and I take care of my girlfriend."

"What do you mean?"

"As my girlfriend, you'll find out. That's why going out with me this weekend will be good for both of us."

"Going out with you? I thought we were just going to find a Christmas tree this weekend."

"Yeah, we're going to do that, but we're also going out. I have somewhere I want to take you on Saturday, and we can grab dinner too."

Arching my eyebrows, I prompt, "Don't you think you should ask me first?"

Chuckling, he does as I request. "Pixie, will you spend the weekend with me?"

A giggle escapes. "You're going from dinner and picking out a Christmas tree to spending the weekend?"

Shrugging, he reiterates, "We already live together."

"All right, Kelly, you have me for the weekend." The words slip out before I have a chance to think it through. My heart is already leaping while my head is trying to tell it to slow down. "Where are we going?"

"I'll tell you when we get there. I promise, you'll like it."

"How can you promise that?"

Leaning closer he looks me in the eyes, holding my gaze. "Because you've caught my eye and I've been paying attention to you, Pixie. I already know you better than you think I do. Trust me."

My heart stutters and my stomach somersaults off a cliff. What is he doing to me? I'm already done for and we haven't even begun. "Okay," I barely squeak out the word.

Chapter 9

Sloane

The moment I step through the door after work, a savory aroma hits my senses. I hang up my purse and kick off my shoes, dragging my exhausted body towards the kitchen to find the source. With my eyes at half mast, I inhale deeply and turn the corner, finding a stockpot of something simmering, but no sign of Kelly. Approaching the stove, I lift the lid and moan in appreciation at the mix of spices.

"I thought I heard you come in," Kelly's deep voice hits me low in my belly from the doorway.

Spinning towards him, my eyes widen as I take him in, leaning against the door frame. Once again, he's barefoot looking sexy as hell, dressed in dark jeans and a sage green t-shirt, clinging to his muscles. He gives me a crooked smile underneath his scruff, a little thicker than his normal five-o-clock shadow. "Hi."

He gestures to the stove. "I made chili and I was waiting for you."

"That's three nights in a row you've made dinner and waited for me. Are you going for a gold star?"

Chuckling, he shrugs. "From you? I'll take whatever kind of reward you want to give me."

I giggle. "This smells so good." My stomach growls as if in agreement.

"I think that means it's time to eat. I'm hungry too," he says, reaching for the bowls. "I've got these if you want to grab drinks."

I do as he suggested and we meet at the table. Grabbing a spoon, I dig in. My mouth closes over a large bite and I close my eyes, savoring the flavors. Swallowing, I open my eyes and find Kelly staring at me, his eyes full of heat. "This is delicious," I say, my voice catching. Clearing my throat, I ask, "Every night you surprise me. How'd you get to be such a good cook?"

A smile tugs at his lips. "My Gram. When I would be home, I used to try to spend as much time with her as my parents would allow. And a lot of our time together was spent in the kitchen. She said one day I'd appreciate it when I could cook for a woman."

An irrational surge of jealousy runs through me. "Have you cooked for a lot of women?"

"No. My Gram, my mom and you," he admits, giving me a hesitant smile.

My heart clenches. "So, you think that will impress me?"

He arches his eyebrows in challenge. "I hope."

"Yeah, you're right, it does," I concede, my cheeks heating.

His grin grows, his eyes sparkling. "I thought we could talk favorites tonight."

"Favorite things? I can do that."

"I was thinking more favorite positions, but we can start with yours and work our way up to mine. He wiggles his eyebrows giving me a salacious grin and I burst out laughing.

"We'll see. Okay, favorite color?" I ask.

"Blue," he answers, "but I already know yours is pink and since I made dinner, I'm supposed to go first, so I get two questions."

"Who the hell made those rules?"

Smirking, he shrugs, "I didn't make the rules, I just play the game."

Giving him an exaggerated sigh, I reluctantly agree, "Sure, whatever you say."

"Favorite dessert."

"Hmm...berries dipped in dark chocolate." I lick my lips.

He groans, wiping his hand down his face. "Okay, moving on..."

"What about yours?"

He gives me a sexy grin and my body ignites instantly. Chuckling, he lets me off the hook and prods, "Favorite guilty pleasure."

"Um...watching reality TV shows."

He quirks a brow. "Huh. That one surprises me. I'd watch with you."

My eyes widen. "You would?"

"Sure. But I'll admit, I was hoping you'd say something about pink vibrators." He winks and my entire body bursts into flames. I swear he's doing that on purpose.

"I'm never going to live that down, am I?"

"You say that like it's a bad thing."

Ignoring his comment, I push forward. "What about you?"

"Watching Christmas movies."

"But those are usually romance movies." He shrugs, gaging me for my reaction, but I'm not sure what to think. Does that mean he's not the player I think he is? Exhaling harshly, I try not to think about it, instead finding out more about him. "Okay, my turn. Favorite place to visit?"

"My Gram's." My heart stops. This man. That's the last answer I expected to come out of his mouth. He's wrapping himself around my heart with just a few simple questions. This is a dangerous game. "What's yours?"

Clearing my throat, I look down at my food and focus on my answer, "So there's this field a couple miles out of the east end of town that has beautiful wildflowers in the late spring and early summer. A small canal trickles in at this one spot. There you can sit listening to the wind blowing through the grass and the trees, the water running downstream, and the birds chirping, while staring out at an array of colorful flowers, breathing in their fresh, floral scent. It's absolutely beautiful, peaceful, and serene. I've never seen anything like it."

Lifting my head, I meet his intense gaze, his stare holding me captive, causing my stomach to flip flop. "Will you bring me there when it's the right time to see it how you picture it? Like six months or so, right?" With my insides in complete chaos over Kelly, I nod my head, wondering if he's just saying that or if he really will be around to join me in the field. My heartbeat picks up its pace at the thought, suddenly hopeful, when that might be the last thing I need, especially since he's only pretending to be my boyfriend.

"Sure," I agree, refusing to think too much about the possibility and take another bite of chili. If he keeps playing my heart so well, I'm going to be consumed by the avalanche that is Kelly before we even make it to Christmas.

Chapter 10

Kelly

The rest of the week flies by, work at the site keeps me busy, but I've been enjoying dinner every night with Sloane. Seeing her is now the highlight of my day. She has a way of bringing a smile to my face that's unfamiliar at best. It feels good to have someone to come home to, even if she's not really mine. But do I want her to be? Would she even take a chance on me? Unsure, I move forward with our original plan knowing this gives us more time and at the same time keeps my family at bay.

Tugging on a pair of faded blue jeans, I run my hand through my damp hair and open the bathroom door, stepping right into Sloane. "Pixie."

Her hand comes down on my bare chest, igniting the heat between us. "Oh, um, sorry, Kelly."

"Don't ever be sorry for touching me." Her tongue juts out, licking her lips before she sucks her lower lip between her teeth. Reaching up, I brush my thumb over her mouth, tugging gently. Hooking my hand behind her neck, I beg, "Please stop doing that unless you're ready for me to push you up against the wall and devour you."

Lifting her gaze, she stares at me. Her eyes flare, and her mouth goes round refreshing my dirty thoughts. I stare, watching her breath pick up its pace causing my heart to race and my dick to jump. "Oh." Licking her lips, she moves closer, the heat of her body heavy on my chest. Without further thought, my fingers flex, pulling her to me, closing the distance between us.

Our lips crash together as she links her arms around my neck, pulling herself closer. She jumps up, wrapping her legs around my waist, while I bring one hand under her jean covered ass with her heated core just above me. I flip her around, pressing her up against the wall by her bedroom door, my good intentions thrown out the window.

Her tongue tangles with mine pulling a moan from her mouth. My body is on fire, ready to explode. Tearing my lips away from hers, I kiss along her jaw, lick, and kiss down her neck, sucking gently as I reach her shoulder, covered by a thin cranberry sweater with a deep V-neck showing off her cleavage. "Fuck me." My hand slips under her sweater, skimming her side and cupping her breast, my thumb running over her already pert nipple.

She gasps. "Kelly, wait." Her words stop me cold. Removing my hand, I set her down and step back awkwardly, my dick as hard as granite. "I'm sorry I–"

"Don't ever apologize for that with me. You need to stop, we stop. But I think I've made it clear that I want you, Sloane and if I haven't, I'm making it known now. But I'm not pushing you into doing something you're not ready for."

"It's not like that."

"It's exactly like that and that's okay, but here's the deal—It's safe to say that I want you every minute of every damn day, so if you decide you're on the same page as me, you need to be the one to make the move. Got it?"

She nods. "Got it."

"Good. Let's get ready to go."

Her lips flicker and my eyes narrow. "Um, I'm ready, but it looks like you forgot your shirt."

Chuckling, I ask, half-serious, "I don't have time for another shower?"

Her head falls back in laughter, the airy sound sending a shiver down my spine. "Get your shirt and let's go."

"Okay." Stepping into my room, I grab a dark green long sleeved t-shirt, yanking it over my head. Returning to her, I urge, "Let's go."

After a half-hour of Sloane and I talking music, concerts we've been to and flipping through stations, we pull into a dirt parking lot at a Christmas tree farm. Stepping out of my truck, I take a deep breath, enjoying the crisp fifty degree weather, cooler than normal for December, but it adds to the atmosphere, making it feel a little more like Christmas.

Sloane is already out of the car by the time I reach her. Taking her hand, I weave our fingers together. She tilts her head, looking up at me, a smile tugging at her lips as we walk side by side towards rows of trees. "Have you ever come here before?" I inquire, hoping this place doesn't come with bad memories. I probably should've asked sooner.

She nods. "Yeah, but it's been a while. We got our Christmas trees here when I was a kid, before my parents split. I haven't been back since."

My nerves suddenly make an appearance, turning my stomach. I stuff my free hand in my pocket. "Ah, is it okay we're here? I don't want–"

"It's great, Kelly. My brother and I used to love coming here. I think it's time. This was always a good memory. I wouldn't be here if it weren't for you, so thank you."

Nodding, I relax. Stepping towards her, I give her a hug and kiss her on her forehead in support. Holding her hand a little tighter, I smile down at her. "Let's go find a tree then."

"Don't we need an ax to cut it down first?"

"No, they don't let people do that here anymore."

"Oh. That changed."

"Disappointed?"

"Probably safer." She giggles, shaking her head as we weave through the trees, the scent of pine strong. It doesn't take long before she points to a Douglas Fir, about seven feet, but not too full. "What about this one?"

"I like it and if it's the one you want, it's ours."

She grins, her eyes sparkling. "Ours," she whispers as if the word itself is a gift. Leaning down, I brush my lips over hers, her smile widening as I pull back.

"Kelly? What are you doing here?" Meg's voice grates over my skin. Turning around, I face her, holding Sloane's hand tight.

"Picking out a Christmas tree with my girlfriend."

She scoffs. "You're dating Sloane?"

"She's the reason I'm staying in Genesis Beach. You two know each other?"

"Yeah," Meg answers.

"Unfortunately," Sloane mumbles under her breath only loud enough for me to hear.

Coughing, I cover my laugh and clear my throat as one of the workers glances down our row. I wave him over, directing him towards our tree. "Enjoy your weekend, Meg."

She pastes on a smile. "Yeah, you too. I'll see you later."

We're halfway home before Sloane blurts out, "How is this supposed to even work? No one is going to believe us. Why would they?"

"What are you talking about?"

She scrunches up her face in disgust. "Meg didn't believe it."

"No, she did."

"If she did, she thinks you're a rebound or you're cheating on me. Either way, I look like an idiot."

"No, she's pissed because she asked me out more than once and I turned her down."

"She probably saw you leave with that woman you came home with the day you moved in." She winces. "This was a bad idea."

"No one saw me leave with anyone. I promise. But do you care what she thinks?"

"Not really, but if we can't even convince her, how are we supposed to convince our families and friends, or my ex?"

I park my truck and unbuckle my seatbelt, turning to face her. "All we have to do is enjoy being together and everyone will believe it, just like she did." That's what I'm doing.

She sucks her bottom lip into her mouth, likely overthinking. Cradling her face in my hands, I hold her gaze before sealing my mouth over hers and moving soft and slow, wanting her to know how precious she is. Pulling back, I lean my forehead on hers insisting, "It's going to be okay. We've got this. Trust me."

"I'm not sure how, but I do."

I press my lips to hers once again, not wanting to stop, but force myself to pull away. "Good. Now, let's go decorate our Christmas tree."

Her eyes brighten, letting me know I'm doing the right thing.

Chapter 11

Kelly

My stomach churns as I run my hands over the steering wheel, glancing at Sloane out of the corner of my eye. I hope I got this right. Her eyes go wide as I pull into the long dirt drive. "What are we doing at the Sagerton place? Are we even allowed to be here?"

Chuckling, I nod. "Yeah, it's okay that we're here. This is the local project I'm working on."

"Wait," she gasps. "What are you talking about? How have we never talked about this? You work in construction?"

"Not exactly. I'm an architect. I'm handling the remodel for the property, including a new guesthouse on the back lot."

"Wow," she murmurs in awe as she climbs out of the truck. I watch Sloane while she's taking everything in, a small smile tugging at her lips. "I always thought this place was so beautiful."

"It is."

"I can picture the driveway with cobblestone at the end and lining the sides leading to a large circle in front of the house with a symbol that means something to the family in the center like a fountain or a tree with benches and seashells crushed and sealed into the cement surrounding it. And there has to be a large weeping willow tree in the front yard with a swing hanging from it." Her excitement increases as she talks, every word from her lips captivating me. "Maybe some privet near the road for privacy. I wonder what kinds of flowers they like. The gardens could be incredible. And depending on what they want to do with the back, there are millions of options." Suddenly, her mouth snaps shut and her face falls.

"What's wrong?" I ask, stepping towards her, my eyebrows drawn in concern.

Shaking her head, she insists, "Nothing."

"Pixie, you lit up talking about what you would do to this place, and you barely scratched the surface. Tell me what you're thinking that made that beautiful look fall from your face."

Scrunching her nose up adorably, she admits, "It's not my project. I don't have a say in anything."

Taking another step closer, I reach for her, my finger hooking under her chin and tipping it up until she meets my gaze. "What if it could be yours?"

Her eyes widen and her breath hitches. "What do you mean?"

"Well, let's just say, I may have some pull, and I know for a fact they still need a landscape designer."

"You don't work with one already?"

"Personally, I've worked with a few on different projects, but this is your town. You know what grows well and what things could work here. Plus, I know you've been wanting to get your hands dirty with a project like this."

"And you don't want to bring someone in with more experience? This is a really big project."

"I'd rather work with you if we can. Pixie, I think we would have a lot of fun together. I could show you my plans so you're able to incorporate your ideas with what everything will look like when it's done."

"Kelly," she rasps. Tears brim her eyelids, and she sucks her bottom lip between her teeth.

My eyebrows draw down in confusion. "I'm sorry if I overstepped, Sloane. I thought this was something you wanted."

She spins back towards me, jumping into my arms making me stumble back a step before I catch my balance. The moment my legs are under me, her lips are on mine. She kisses me hard. Her lips move over mine, frenzied. I wrap my arms around her, holding her close as she arches her body into mine making my dick swell and my breath catch.

Pulling back, she looks at me with a wide grin and bright eyes causing my heart to skip a beat. "I've never wanted something so bad in my life, but I didn't even know who to contact to put my name in. This is incredible, Kelly. Thank you for a chance to do this!"

"You're welcome."

She gives me another chaste kiss before sliding down my body prompting me to groan. "I need to go work on my proposal. When do I need to have something prepared?" She steps away from me and begins pacing. "Oh, my gosh, I should take pictures and then we should go. I need measurements and can I see your plans? I have so much work to do."

Chuckling, I hold my hands up. "Slow down, Pixie, slow down. You have time. I promise."

"Are you sure?"

Grabbing her around the waist, I tug her into my chest. My fingers graze her sides, sliding up. Cradling her face in my hands, I insist, "I'm sure." Tipping my head down, I brush my lips over hers. "How about I show you around and then we go grab something to eat?"

"Yes, please."

"You know this town better than me, Pixie. So where would you like to go for dinner?"

"What about Mackie's? It's down on the water. It's casual with good food and a fantastic view."

"Sounds good, but I already have the view I want right here." She blushes, giving me exactly what I was going for.

"You were right, by the way," she says, swiftly changing the subject.

"I'm right?" A cocky grin tugs at my lips making her giggle.

"Today is perfect."

"Good." Weaving my fingers into her hair, I press my lips to hers again, kissing her soft and slow. Every move, every touch igniting me to my core and pulling me in deep. I want this. I want her.

Taking a deep breath, I pull back and smile down at her. She grins, but in the next moment sucks her bottom lip into her mouth, giving me her tell. She's still over thinking us. Time to show her around before I do something I shouldn't when she still doesn't seem to be ready for more. I just hope she gives me the chance to change her mind.

Chapter 12

Sloane

We walk up to Mackie's, listening to the waves crash against the shore, the soothing sound bringing a smile to my face. The wreath adorned with jingle bells rings as we step inside pushing the door closed behind us. Gesturing to the ocean, I proclaim, "Being close to the water is definitely one of my favorite things about living here. Well, that along with not having a hard, bitterly cold winter like up north."

"I agree with you there." Kelly nods.

Looking around, we admire the Christmas decorations, strewn about the entire restaurant. A small wreath hangs on a post above the square, reclaimed wood bar in the middle of the restaurant, with garland wrapped with lights completely surrounding it. High-top tables encompass the bar, already full of patrons, and many familiar faces.

James, one of the managers stands behind the bar, swiftly moving from one thing to the next, making it look effortless.

The tall wooden booths along the perimeter looking out at the beach have sprigs of pine and pinecones in between each booth with mistletoe hanging at the top of each window, garland looping them all together and Christmas music playing softly through the overhead speakers.

"Hi. Two for dinner?" A woman asks.

"Yes, please," Kelly answers before I register her question.

"Right this way," she advises, leading us to a booth along the windows. She sets the menus on the table and smiles. "Hannah will be right with you."

"Thank you," I say, sliding into the booth.

Hannah steps up to our table with a wide smile, her petite and curvy form bouncing with joy. "Sloane, hi! I haven't seen you since…" she winces trailing off and falling back on her heels. "It's, ah, good to see you."

Brushing it off, I give her a genuine smile, refusing to let Dan and Fiona get in my head. Today has been perfect. Hannah is three years younger than me, but we were in a couple clubs together my senior year of high school and we've remained friendly. She's a sweetheart. "Hi, Hannah. It's good to see you too. How have you been?"

"Good. Busy here." She laughs.

"Oh, I'm sorry. Hannah, this is Kelly."

They turn towards each other, smiling and making my stomach twist. Like me, she hates all the attention she gets from her body, but I haven't seen many guys who don't look–she's beautiful. "Hi, Hannah.

I'm Sloane's new boyfriend," he declares, keeping his eyes on her face before veering back to me, winking.

My face heats, but I relax in my seat, grinning. He's nothing like the man I used to date.

"New boyfriend? That's fantastic! It's so nice to meet you." Pausing, she glances in my direction, blushing. "No offense, but your ex is a jerk."

Kelly's head falls back in laughter as I agree, "You're right, Hannah. I'm lucky. I definitely traded up."

"I'm not going to argue with you, but I got the best deal out of his stupidity."

"Awe," she croons. "That's so sweet. I guess I should get back to work and ask if y'all know what you want to order to drink?"

I giggle. "May I have a water and whatever light beer you have on tap?" She nods.

"I'll have the same," Kelly answers. "Thanks."

He watches me smiling as she walks away. "A lot of people think your ex was an asshole?"

"Honestly, I don't know. But I don't care anymore either. He's not my problem." Christmas at my dad's flashes in my mind, but it doesn't kill my mood like it normally would. "Thank you, Kelly."

His eyebrows draw down in confusion. "For what?"

"Everything." I laugh. "For today. For moving in with me. For getting me to decorate our place for Christmas. For spending Christmas with me. Thank you for all of it."

He reaches across the table, grabs my hand and squeezes. "I wouldn't want to be anywhere else."

My heart lurches, getting caught in my throat. I swallow hard and tear my eyes from his. "Um, everything is really good here, but I think I'm in the mood for a cheeseburger. What do you think?"

Not even bothering to pick up a menu, he states, "I think I'm in the mood for whatever you're having."

"And maybe if you're good we'll have dessert," I tease, realizing what I said the moment the words leave my lips. Gasping my eyes widen, my free hand flying up and covering my mouth.

"Fuck me," he mumbles under his breath, his eyes flaring, the heat between us instantly palpable.

Straightening, I lean forward. Feigning confidence, I quietly proclaim, "If I can make it through you badgering me about my panties and my vibrator, you can survive through a little talk about dessert."

"You just might be the death of me, Pixie," he grumbles. He stares at me, running his hand down his face, and along his jaw making me giggle. Shrugging, he adds, "I have to admit, it would be worth it for you."

My cheeks heat, flushing as he turns the tables once again just as Hannah sets our drinks down in front of us. "Have y'all decided what you want to order for dinner?" she asks.

"Yes," I nod ordering a cheeseburger and fries, Kelly doing the same. Unfortunately, the rest of the evening flies by all too quickly.

Disappointment hits me as we walk in the door, knowing our weekend is over. Although, living together makes the end of our date awkward, or maybe it's just me feeling that way. "So, um, thank you again for today. I had a great time. I guess I'll see you in the morning."

"Going to bed already, Pixie? It's only nine and I haven't seen you go to bed before eleven since I moved in."

"No, but what am I supposed to do? This is the first time I've been on a date with a guy who's not really my boyfriend and he doesn't leave at the end of the night. I'm not like you, I'm not a one-night stand kind of woman."

"No, you're not and that's a good thing. You're the kind of woman any man would want to stick around."

My lips tug upwards. "Thanks."

He nods. "A man can change for the right woman, you know."

I arch my eyebrows in question, my breath catching. "What are you saying, Kelly?"

"Maybe you're the right woman for me."

My heart pounds, blood rushing in my ears, wondering if he means what he's saying. Stepping closer, I wrap my hands around his neck, tugging his head towards me as I push up on my tiptoes. "You think so?" I ask, my heated breath on his mouth, filled with desire.

"I do, but I'm trying to confirm my theory." Our lips meet in the middle, moving together slowly, melding together in a perfect rhythm, making me moan.

Pulling back, breathless, I ask, "How do you propose we do that?"

"Oh, I have plenty of ideas, but I don't know if you're ready for them; ready for me–yet."

Tugging him closer, I kiss him harder, joined in a slow steady dance. My body vibrates with need, yet I can't help but question my desire. Falling back on my heels, our lips break apart, our breaths heaving. "I think you're right. I need to get my head on straight first."

Nodding, he gives me a chaste kiss, his finger hooked under my chin. He pulls back, looking into my eyes, insisting, "Do what you need to do. I'll be right here, Pixie. I'm not going anywhere."

My heart clenches while my head spins, hoping his words are true and wondering if I should take the chance.

"Thank you, Kelly. Goodnight."

"Goodnight."

Questions spin in my head, the biggest–should I believe in him or run?

Chapter 13

Kelly

"Thanks for getting these changes to us so quickly, Kelly," Gordon states, reaching out his hand to shake mine.

"No problem. I know what an asshole the owner can be." I smirk.

Gordon laughs. "You and me both."

I shake my head in amusement as I feel my phone ring in my pocket. "Sloane will be coming in with her proposal on Friday. Let me know what you need from me for that meeting." He nods.

At the mention of her name, my thoughts inevitably drift to her. It has been a few days since Sloane and I spent the weekend together. Since we've been back, it feels like she's been avoiding me. She claims it's only because she's working on her proposal for the Sagerton property in all of her free time and she can't focus when she's around me, likely because I keep asking questions. That may be partially true, although I can't help but wonder if she's second guessing our deal or reconsidering giving us a chance.

"Kelly," Meg calls as I pass by her desk.

I hate that she works at the local contractor's office, making it so I have no way of avoiding her. "Afternoon, Meg. Do you need something?"

"No, I just wanted to check in to see how you're doing. I don't get to talk to you anymore since you moved here." She sticks out her bottom lip.

"That's because I'm here and can do my work directly, but I appreciate you delivering messages when I can't be." Offering her a fake smile, I turn to leave the office.

"Oh, I almost forgot, I have a message for you from your roommate."

My breath catches in my throat, and I turn facing her. "Sloane called here? What's wrong? Is she okay?"

"She sounded fine to me, she just said to call her. Apparently, you weren't answering her calls. If there's trouble between you two," she begins stepping towards me, her hand barely touching my arm and prompting me into motion.

"Thanks," I call as I run out the door, Meg's frustrated sigh hitting my ears before the door slams.

Jogging to my truck, I pull out my phone, tapping Sloane's name. "Kelly, thank God! I've been trying to call you."

"What's wrong?" I ask as I start my truck.

"I don't know, but I'm here at the hospital."

"Hospital?" I echo, turning in that direction.

"Yes, but they won't tell me anything because I'm not family."

"You're okay." I breathe a sigh of relief, the moment short lived. "Wait. What are you talking about?"

"Your grandma." My heart stops. "The assisted living facility called me since they couldn't get in touch with you, but only to find you. They won't tell me anything. No one will."

"I'm on my way," I declare, my voice raw.

"Please, drive safe, Kelly."

"I will." Disconnecting, I toss my phone on the seat. I just need to get there. My mind races with all the possibilities, panic setting in as I pull into the parking lot in record time and park my truck. Jumping out, I run towards the entrance and crash into the front desk. "Lilith Travers."

"Kelly," Sloane says my name as her hand falls to my back in support, the simple action comforting.

"Are you family?" the woman behind the desk asks.

"Yes, I'm her grandson and emergency contact, Kelly Travers."

She types into her computer and nods. "Okay, you can go back, but we prefer only family in the ER."

Snagging Sloane's hand, I insist, "She is family."

The woman purses her lips but gives us what we need. "She's through the double doors to the right in bay six. I'll buzz you through."

"Thank you," Sloane says while I tug her along behind me.

We quickly find the curtained off area and I peek inside, breathing a sigh of relief the moment I see her sitting up in bed. "Gram."

"Kelly." She smiles. "What are you doing here?"

"The assisted living facility called. What happened?" I ask, reaching for her hand with my free one.

"I'm fine, I just fell." She waves me off, her smile broadening when her gaze settles on Sloane. "And who is this?"

"Gram, this is Sloane, my girlfriend."

"Hi," Sloane whispers.

Gram claps her hands in excitement before wincing. "Be careful." I reach towards her, attempting to settle her back in bed.

"Kelly, I'm fine."

"Humor me."

She sighs and reaches out with her free hand towards Sloane. She steps closer to the bed, grasping my grandmother's hand, the sight squeezing my heart. "You're a beautiful woman."

Sloane blushes making her even more stunning. "Thank you."

Gram looks back and forth between us and nods her head. "Of course, I've heard so many wonderful things about you over the years and I can already tell she's good for you."

Chuckling, I nod in agreement. "You're right as usual."

"Over the years?" Sloane asks, her eyebrows drawn down in confusion.

Gram waves away her concern. "We live in a very small town sweetheart. So, Sloane, I want to know everything about you." Gram begins, just as a young doctor walks into the cubicle.

"Hello, Mrs. Travers. I see you have visitors," the doctor says, his eyes running over Sloane. I don't blame him, but I release my grandmother's hand and step back, my arm going possessively around Sloane's shoulders. He clears his throat and asks, "Would you like them to step out while we talk?"

"No, they can stay. This is my grandson and his girlfriend."

He turns to us, smiling. "Hi, I'm Dr. Hull and I actually have some good news for your grandmother." He focuses back on her and states, "You have no broken bones. Although, there is some definite swelling on your knee, so I'm going to ask you to stay off of it for a few days. Your bruising may get worse before it gets better, but you will be feeling like yourself again in no time. In the meantime, let's stick to Tylenol for any pain."

"Okay, thank you, Doctor." She smiles.

Exhaling in relief, I murmur my appreciation. "Thank you."

"You're welcome." He nods, keeping his focus on my grandmother. "Do you have any questions?"

"You answered everything. I'm ready to go."

"Okay. I'll have a nurse come in with your discharge paperwork in a few minutes. Please be more careful next time. It was nice meeting you." He glances at Sloane one more time before slipping out.

"See? I'm fine. Now let's break out of this popsicle stand."

I laugh, tension leaving my shoulders. A few minutes later the nurse steps into the room. "I can help get your grandmother ready to leave if y'all want to step outside."

Sloane and I nod in agreement. "Thank you," I mumble as we slip out through the curtains.

"Are you okay?" she whispers.

Tugging Sloane to a stop, I look into her eyes needing her to know how big this was for me. "Thanks to you. Thank you."

"You don't have to thank me, Kelly, I'm just glad she's okay. I'm sorry I didn't have more information for you when I talked to you."

"There's no reason to apologize. I have all these missed calls, and I had no idea. When I moved into town, I gave them your number as my backup. I'm sorry I didn't even warn you."

"That doesn't matter."

"Oh, it matters. Thank you for finding me. I can't..." Tipping my head down, I brush my mouth across her lips, resting my forehead on hers." Just–thank you."

"You're welcome," she whispers, her voice cracking.

She doesn't even know it, but I'm already hers.

I'm finally able to breathe when Sloane helps me get my grandmother settled in my truck. "Thank you, dear. You're good for my boy." Sloane turns a deep shade of red, remaining silent. "Will you be coming with Kelly on Christmas Eve to see me?"

"Oh, I don't know," she answers knowing that wasn't part of our deal, but I don't care.

"I sure hope so," I claim, holding her gaze.

"Then, I will be there."

"Wonderful." Gram smiles, reaching up to give Sloane a hug.

The way Sloane relaxes into her embrace turns my stomach into knots. Sloane stands, waving. "I'll see you at home," I tell her, the unfamiliar words seeming so natural.

Relaxing back in my seat, I pull away from the hospital, feeling my grandmother's eyes on me.

"So, your roommate is now your girlfriend? I have to admit, I'm surprised you listened."

I wince, not able to lie to her. "I wouldn't say I listened, exactly."

"What would you say?"

"She's kind of a fake girlfriend."

"Kelly," she admonishes, guilt washing over me.

"I'm sorry I wasn't completely honest."

"Explain," she demands.

My fingers tap against the steering wheel. I don't talk about women I'm dating, but there hasn't been a single one I wanted to introduce to the woman sitting beside me, until now. Although, this wasn't the way I wanted it to happen.

The last few hours run through my mind like a train wreck, grateful Gram is okay.

Taking a deep breath, I gather the courage to tell her the truth. "I asked Sloane if she would come to mom and dad's Christmas party with me as my girlfriend and I would go to her family Christmases with her as her boyfriend, but it's not real."

She bursts out laughing." If that's not real, Kelly, then bury me now because there's nothing more real and worth living for than the way the two of you look at each other."

"Gram!"

She heaves a sigh. "You are nothing like your parents. Don't let their relationship deter you from having something special. Sloane is worth it."

A smile tugs at my lips. "You're right, Gram. She's beautiful inside and out. I've been falling for her since the day I met her, but I don't know if she feels the same."

"Oh, I've heard you say this before, so I'll ask you. You're a grown-ass man, so what's holding you back?"

"Pretty sure I'm in my own way." I chuckle. "You don't think living with her complicates things?"

"Nah, just makes it easier when you stay together because you will, Kelly. I'm sure of it."

Chapter 14

Sloane

Bursting through the front door, I call out in excitement, "Kelly, I'm home! Are you here?"

He steps out from the kitchen with a glass of water in his hand and meets my gaze, arching his eyebrows in question. "How'd it go?" he asks, setting the glass on the table as he passes.

"I got the job!"

Grinning wide, he steps towards me and wraps me in his arms, swinging me around. "Congratulations! I'm so happy for you!"

He sets me on my feet, keeping his hands planted on my waist. "You were right, they loved my plans. I can't believe I'm going to be able to work on this project. This is like a dream come true."

"You deserve this, Pixie."

"Thank you. I appreciate all your notes. They really helped everything come together for me. I was able to use them to come up with the perfect plan."

"Sounds like it. We should celebrate."

My face falls. "I would love to, but if you still want me to come to your parents party next weekend, I should probably get some rest and then go shopping tomorrow. I still don't have a dress."

Pursing his lips, he gets a look on his face I can't quite decipher. "Yeah, um, about that..."

My stomach drops. Does he have another date? Maybe he thinks we're a bad idea. Does that mean he's not coming with me for Christmas? What am I going to do about my family? I don't want to face Dan and Fiona alone now that I've gotten used to the idea of him coming with me. "Is something wrong?"

Shaking his head, he attempts to quickly reassure me. "No, no, nothing like that."

"Then, what is it?"

He runs his hand over his jaw, keeping his eyes on me. "Well, you've been pretty busy this week working on the proposal. I didn't want you to have to worry about my parents party when you're doing me a favor."

"You're doing me one too, at least I think you are."

"I wouldn't miss Christmas if that's what you're asking."

"Thanks, Kelly. So, what did you do?"

"I had Gordon ask your friend, Alex, what size dress you wear, and I got you something."

My mouth drops open in shock. "What?"

"Hopefully, you like the dress, but I think you'll look incredible in it, and I wanted to do something for you to say thank you."

"Wait. You bought me a dress?"

"Yeah, I hope I didn't overstep. You don't have to wear it if you don't want to."

My heart stutters. No one has ever done something like that for me before. It feels like something out of the movies. I wonder what it looks like. "Thank you."

"Do you want to see it?"

"I'd love to." He grins, his shoulders relaxing. Taking me by the hand, he leads me down the short hallway, opening the door to his room.

"Close your eyes," he advises. So, I do.

He lets go of my hand and I listen to him shuffling around the room. A moment later he takes my hand again and instructs, "Okay, open them."

My eyes flutter open, and my gaze meets his, the look on his face both sheepish and hopeful causing my heart to lodge itself in my throat. He nods towards the bed. Turning my head, I gasp, my eyes widening at the strapless, shimmering, green gown embedded with emerald beading in intricate floral patterns on the bodice and sweeping along the bottom. Stepping towards the bed, I run my hands along the fabric, soft and silky to the touch. "This is beautiful, Kelly."

"You like it?"

"I love it. The details remind me of your eyes."

Chuckling, he claims, "Ironically, it reminded me of you, Pixie."

"Why?" I ask, curious.

"Your love for landscape design, and the passion in the way you talk about everything."

Looking away from the dress, I stare at him, my eyes wide. He has no way of knowing how much he struck a nerve. "Passion?"

"It's why I call you Pixie. From the moment I met you, you don't back down from anything. You get this fire in your eyes when you're excited or challenged or defiant, or when you love something. I see it when I look at you and in the way you talk. It's one of the most beautiful things about you."

My heart thunders in my chest, ready to burst. Without a second thought, I reach up, wrapping my arms around his neck. Pushing up on my tiptoes, I tug his head towards mine and press my lips to his, kissing him with everything in me.

Our lips move together, seeking a rhythm all their own. We swiftly find our way together. His tongue runs over my lip, begging for entrance. I open, willingly, giving it to him. Tongues tangling, twisting, licking, tasting, exploring. I can't get enough. My hands roam the hard ridges of his body.

His lips fall to my neck, his tongue jutting out and licking sensitive spots on my skin. One hand slides down my side, gliding over my front, my body arching towards him. "Fuck," he mumbles, his hard cock pressing into my stomach. "Every piece of me wants you, Sloane."

"Please," I beg, falling back onto his bed next to the dress with his lips following. His hand slips underneath my shirt, his thumb grazing my belly as he makes his way towards my chest. Palming my breast, his thumb runs over my taut nipple making me gasp, and my body burn. Slowly, he leaves a trail of kisses down my body. Heat pools between my legs, his hand inching down my thigh. "Touch me, please."

"Tell me where, Pixie."

"Between my legs."

"Do you mean here?" he asks as he kisses me below my bellybutton.

"Lower."

"What about here?" he asks, brushing his lips along my upper thigh and eliciting a whimper from my lips.

"Kelly, please."

His heated breath over my panties makes me groan. My body arches towards him and my hands weave into his hair and tug him towards my core making him chuckle. Inhaling deeply, he moans, "Damn, you smell good." Hooking his fingers in the sides of my panties, he tugs them down and tosses them to the ground.

Taking his time, he readjusts himself between my legs. Giving me a crooked grin, his eyes sparkle with mischief causing my heart to thrash against my ribcage. "Is this where you want me?" he asks, his finger running through my folds.

Unable to answer, I nod. The next moment, his tongue flattens against me, gliding slow and firm to my clit. He moans, sucking me into his mouth and releasing me, the vibrations driving me wild. "You taste like fucking heaven."

His hot breath between my legs causes me to moan, begging for more, "Please." Kelly slides his tongue up and down my swollen pussy, swirling it around my clit. My body arches towards him and my hands weave into his hair, holding him to me, my actions spurring him on.

Moving his hand around to my ass, he squeezes as his tongue pushes inside, licking to my clit, swirling, sucking, and nibbling. My vision starts to fade and my eyes close. My head falls back while my body arches, desperate to get impossibly closer.

My body heats, and my breathing becomes ragged. Bucking closer, everything deep inside me begins to tingle desperate for a release as I swell around him. Soft humming comes from his lips, the light vibrations pushing me over the edge and making me scream his name. "Kelly!"

Eagerly, his tongue laps up my juices as my body spasms against his mouth and I slowly ride out my orgasm. Spent, my body sags against his mattress, satisfied, with small aftershocks running through me.

"Kelly," I moan his name, gasping for breath. He crawls up my body, kissing my skin as he goes. "You have too many clothes on."

Chuckling, he shakes his head. "Damn, I wish, but we don't have time for more now."

Groaning, I challenge, "Are you sure about that?"

"When you let me inside you, Pixie, I'm not letting you out of this bed, so yeah, I'm sure."

I grin. "Mm. Okay. But you can do that anytime you want."

"Anytime?" Hovering over me, he smirks, wiggling his eyebrows and making me giggle.

"That was...so...good."

"What about fantastic?"

"Sure, I'll give you that and definitely better than my vibrator."

He laughs, tenderly pressing his lips to mine as if he has all the time in the world, the taste of me on his lips. Pulling back, he lays by my side, holding my gaze. "You must know how incredible you are and how much you deserve the best. Doesn't anyone ever tell you?" he questions, guessing exactly what pushed me over the edge and into his arms. "You should hear compliments every single day."

"Sure, people say nice things." I shrug. "But not like that."

A frown mars his lips. "That right there tells me all the men you've had in your life have been assholes. You deserve more, Pixie. So much more."

"Be careful or the guy I first met wouldn't stand a chance with me."

"Then I'm not being careful enough because that man shouldn't have a chance at all, but I'm begging for you to forgive him and give him another chance anyway."

My chest tightens, making it difficult to breathe as I stare at Kelly. "Are you sure you want one?"

"I've never been more sure of anything in my entire life, Pixie. I'll prove it to you if you give me the opportunity."

This almost doesn't feel real, but this isn't something I could make up. "What are you doing to me, Kelly?" I whisper under my breath.

"Apparently not enough."

He's never been more wrong. I'm falling in deep as he exceeds every single one of my expectations I believed I wanted and all of those I never knew I needed.

Chapter 15

Kelly

Busy is an understatement. Spending my time putting out fires is not what I wanted to do this week, but at least we're back on track with renovations.

Dealing with issues on the project did succeed in keeping my mind off my parents and their Christmas party. That's a plus. Hopefully, it won't be as bad as I expect.

Reaching out, I grasp Sloane's hand, helping her out of my truck. With her by my side, I don't care what they throw at me. She's the only thing that matters.

Glancing at her once again, my heart hammers against my ribcage and my mouth goes dry. She might be the death of me. She looks absolutely stunning. The dress clings to her curves, showcasing her beauty. Her hair is pulled up in an elegant twist accented with green and crystal jewels pinned to keep it in place and a few loose tendrils framing her face.

"Is something wrong?" she asks fidgeting with her dress.

Lifting her hand to my lips, I kiss the back of it and look into her eyes. "No. I'm just admiring how beautiful you are and thinking how lucky I am."

"You clean up nice yourself," she claims, blushing a deep shade of red.

Smoothing out my black tuxedo jacket with my free hand, I glance up the circular drive. "Thanks." She straightens my emerald tie, matching her dress. "And thank you for coming with me."

"Thank you for bringing me."

Huffing a laugh, I claim, "You won't be saying that by the end of the night, but maybe you'll let me make it up to you."

"Oh?" She quirks her brow, her eyes sparking with the fire I adore. "What do you have in mind?"

My eyes flare while my thoughts instantly plunge into the gutter. "I have lots of ideas and I can be relentless. Guess you'll have to wait to see." With a wink, I tear my gaze away, attempting to readjust without an audience.

"Wow," she murmurs, looking up at my parents' house and taking it in. A massive Victorian with large white pillars along the front porch looking out over a sprawling front lawn, enclosed by a large hedge and an iron front gate with white stone gargoyles perched on each side stands before us. "Did you grow up here?"

I heave a sigh, nodding. "Yeah, but I'm already more at home in Genesis Beach than I ever was here." We drove for less than an hour, but this town is like another world, filled with old money and assholes always trying to one up the other. "This is not my scene."

"But it's your parents."

Grimacing, I concede, "Yeah and no matter how much I try to deny it, I wouldn't be where I am if it weren't for them. Even if it's not what they wanted for me."

"I get it. You're a good man, Kelly." She smirks. "Much better than I first gave you credit for."

Chuckling, I shrug, grateful when she lightens the mood. "I'd already had a few drinks, and you were the one taunting me with panties and vibrators."

She blushes a deep shade of red just as the door opens with my parents' butler standing in the doorway in a black tuxedo. "Good evening, Stuart."

"Master Travers, welcome home." I give him a stiff smile and he nods at Sloane. "Miss, Merry Christmas."

"Merry Christmas." Sloane grins as we step into the white marble foyer.

Garland wrapped with gold ribbon and winter berries adorns the doorways and hangs loosely along the banister. We walk to our left, the living room decorated with the same theme of pine draped with gold along the fireplace and windows. A tall Christmas tree sits in the corner opposite the piano decorated with white lights and gold, silver, and white ornaments, none of them sentimental like the ones I got from my grandmother.

"Kelly," my dad calls from behind me.

Clasping Sloane's hand in mine, I turn, forcing a smile. "Hi, Dad. Nice party."

"The caterers have all the food outside. You," he pauses looking Sloane up and down causing me to tug her closer to my side. Grimacing, he continues, "You and your guest should come outside. There are some people you need to say hello to."

"We will, but Dad, I want to introduce you. This is Sloane, my girlfriend," I emphasize.

Narrowing his eyes, he questions, "Your girlfriend? Your mother said you might bring a date, but she didn't say anything about a girlfriend." Stepping closer he speaks in a hushed tone, "I thought we talked about this. It's time you take this seriously. We have some families here tonight that it would benefit you to get to know better and some women perfectly suited for you."

Clenching my jaw, I take a deep breath, attempting to get my temper under control before I open my mouth. Through gritted teeth, I proclaim, "I am taking this seriously. I'm old enough to know who I want to date and who I'm falling in love with, so you better treat Sloane with some respect or I'll walk out of here with her right now and I won't be back."

Sloane's quick intake of air startles me, making me realize what I said, but I maintain my focus on my dad. He opens his mouth to respond when one of his colleagues steps up behind him and I take it as an opportunity to slip away, pulling Sloane along beside me.

"Kelly," she calls, tugging my hand.

Forcing myself to stop, I give her my full attention. "Are you okay?" I ask, my hand reaching up and gently brushing her cheek.

Arching an eyebrow, she prods, "I'm fine, but I was just about to ask you the same thing."

Huffing a humorless laugh, I shake my head. "Sometimes I wonder why I even bother coming at all. That's only the beginning."

"Your grandmother was wonderful."

A small smile tugs at my lips. "Yeah, she is amazing. You'd like my uncle too."

"Your uncle?"

"Yeah, he owns the bar I met you at."

Her eyes widen. "Your uncle is Ace Morgan? Now, I see it."

Giving her a crooked grin, I nod. "Yeah. There's definitely a family resemblance. He's my mom's brother, but they don't get along." Tipping my head down, I brush my lips over hers, her kiss calming my frustration.

"You can wait until you're in private. You know how I feel about public displays of affection," my mother complains behind my back.

Heaving a sigh, I straighten my back and turn towards her, keeping my arm protectively around Sloane. "Merry Christmas, Mother."

She pastes a smile on her face, holds her hand out and tips her head up, waiting for me to kiss her cheek in greeting. "Merry Christmas, Kelly. It's so nice you could make it home for Christmas. And this must be your girlfriend?" she questions, pursing her lips as she looks Sloane over, not giving anything away.

Nodding, I open my mouth to introduce them, but Sloane beats me to it. "Hi, I'm Sloane and you must be Mrs. Travers. You have a beautiful home."

"Yes, thank you."

"Thank you for having me. It's a wonderful party."

"It is," my mother affirms, assessing Sloane.

Sloane holds a small gift bag up with her free hand that I didn't even realize she was holding. My mother's eyes widen in surprise, a small smile curving her lips. "Merry Christmas." Sloane smiles, handing her the gift. "I wanted to bring you something."

"Thank you, dear." My mother pulls out a small gold frame, hanging from a gold ribbon with a picture of me laughing. It's a picture I didn't realize she even took making my heart squeeze. My mother's gaze softens as she glances from me to Sloane. "Thank you," she reiterates, blinking back tears, surprising me. "So, Sloane, tell me about your family, dear."

"Well, my mom and brother live in Genesis Beach–"

My mother perks up. "Oh, that adorable little beach town where everyone vacations."

"That's where grandma lives too," I remind her.

"Oh, right." She frowns. Waving her hand towards Sloane, she grins, brushing off her reaction. "My mother-in-law never was my biggest fan."

"And your brother," I add, arching my eyebrow.

She clenches her jaw letting me know to back off. "Yes, well, it's been a while. Anyway, keep going, dear."

Hesitant, Sloane glances from me to my mom before continuing. "My dad and his wife–"

"Your parents are divorced?" my mother interrupts her, eyes wide.

"Yes, and my dad is remarried and living one town over."

"Hm. What does he do?"

"He's a manager for the packaging company in Russet."

Her frown deepens. "What about your mom?"

"Enough of the interrogation, Mom," I interrupt, knowing she's judging everything, the gift Sloane brought nearly forgotten. She doesn't care about anything except someone's standing and what it can do for her and I'm not letting her do that to Sloane.

"I'm just trying to get to know her."

"Then ask her questions about herself. She's not her family," I insist, my insinuations clear.

Sloane smiles up at me, laying her hand on my chest. "It's okay, Kelly."

"No, it's not."

My mother sighs and begins scanning the room, a genuine smile lighting up her face as her eyes catch on something behind me. "Oh, look who's here."

My body stiffens and I turn slowly, releasing Sloane's hand as a woman slams into me, throwing her arms around me. I step back, attempting to catch my balance. "Kelly, I missed you!"

"Portia, it's nice to see you." Reaching for her hands, I attempt to untangle her limbs from my body while she gives me a chaste kiss in greeting. I catch a glimpse of Sloane out of the corner of my eye, her eyes alight with amusement, watching me. "I have someone I'd like to introduce you to."

"Oh?" She arches her eyebrow in question, finally moving back and allowing me to breathe.

Extending my hand towards Sloane, she looks down, smirking as if deciding whether or not she should take it. "Pixie," I murmur a playful warning.

Her smile grows, momentarily taking my breath away before she slips her small hand in my large one. Breathing a sigh of relief, I smile and finally meet Portia's gaze as she nearly staggers back, glaring at Sloane. "This is my girlfriend, Sloane."

"Girlfriend," she echoes, silently seething. Pasting on a fake smile, she holds her hand out to Sloane. "Nice meeting you. Kelly and I go way back, but I didn't know he had a girlfriend."

"Oh, probably because we've been so busy since we moved in together," Sloane claims, her eyes sparkling with mischief. "It's so nice to meet one of Kelly's *old* friends."

Portia's mouth drops open. I bite my lip, wanting to laugh and devour Sloane at the same time.

"We were just about to go outside," I say, halting further conversation. "Enjoy your night."

Placing my hand on the small of Sloane's back, my fingertips tingle as I lead her away from my mom and Portia. "For a second there I thought you were just going to laugh at me."

"I almost did, but I felt sorry for you."

Chuckling, I brush my lips over hers. "I'm glad you did. We can leave when you're ready. I feel like I've already overstayed my welcome and I'd have a lot more fun going home and stripping this dress off you."

Sloane turns a deep shade of red making me grin. Her lips twitch, trying to keep a straight face. "Only if I can strip you out of that tux, and then you can make tonight up to me like you promised."

My eyes widen in surprise, relishing her bold words. I press my mouth to hers, mumbling over her lips, "Feel like ordering in?"

Chapter 16

Sloane

This entire week has been a whirlwind. From the Travers over the top Christmas party to starting to work on the landscape design project, to my relationship with Kelly. It doesn't feel like he's just my roommate and my fake boyfriend. We hold hands, we kiss, we touch and talk for hours. He even gives me orgasms that makes my body tremble for days, but we haven't had sex.

It's confusing. I'm not sure if it's just a line he thinks he can't cross with our deal or if he just doesn't want this with me, but if wanting me is the problem, he's not the man I believe he is. Then again, he's been doing and saying a lot of things that make me question if he really is a player. Unfortunately, now my stupid heart is involved, and I can't help but question if any of this is real. Is he just pretending? I'm not even sure if I should give him the gift I bought for him. Will he like it?

Christmas music sounds from the living room, drawing my attention. Taking a deep breath, I gather my courage and make my way out to see Kelly. After all, it is Christmas Eve, and we did say we would spend today together. But now that we're back from seeing his grandmother, I'm starting to wonder if I can keep spending time with him if he doesn't feel this like I do. There's a reason I told Alex I wasn't a one-night stand kind of woman. My heart tends to trip over itself and living with him makes it even more complex.

"There you are. I was wondering where you disappeared to," Kelly says, smiling as he steps towards me.

My heart lurches in response and he just said hello. I'm so screwed. "Yeah, I wanted to get more comfortable."

"You look cute."

"I'm wearing sweatpants," I say in disbelief.

"What's your point? Makes it easier access for me." He gives me a wicked grin and my cheeks heat instantly. "Thank you for coming with me to see my Grandma. She really enjoyed lunch and spending time with us. It actually felt like Christmas for a change."

"It was fun. I'm glad she liked the ornament I made for her."

"She did and believe it or not, my mother liked the gift you gave her the other day too. It's not often she gets emotional. You surprised her and that's not easy to do."

I give him a stiff smile, wrapping my arms around myself. Stepping closer, he reaches for me, his hands resting on my arms. Arching his eyebrow, he asks, "You okay, Pixie?"

Nodding, I give him partial honesty, "Yeah, I'm just tired."

He searches my face for the truth and finally nods, accepting my lame excuse. "Okay. I have a present for you, and we could watch a movie or something if you want?"

"You have a present for me? You've already given me more than enough with the dress."

"That was for doing me a favor. I wanted to get you something for Christmas."

"Oh." My heart lodges itself in my throat and I attempt to gulp it down, my eyes glued to Kelly.

A smile tugs at his lips. I watch as he steps over to the Christmas tree and bends down, picking up a small box and a larger one. "Sit down so you can open them," he suggests, excitement shining in his eyes.

Lowering myself onto the couch, I tuck my legs up underneath me. He sits next to me, handing me the boxes. "Thank you."

Tearing into the first box, I blink back my tears. A large sketch pad and colored pencils sit in the box.

"I know you probably already have these, but I figured since you haven't been able to do much designing lately you might like something new."

Looking into his eyes, my heart lurches. "This is perfect. Thank you."

Smiling, he places his hand on my knee, sending a shock right through me. "You're welcome."

Needing to get my emotions under control, I rip the red and white paper off the small box and flip open a black velvet jewelry box. A soft gasp slips from my lips. Picking up the delicate gold necklace, I admire the two daisies hanging from it with the stems intertwined and tiny diamonds in the center of each daisy. A tiny golden fairy sits on the stems, holding them together making my stomach twist into knots. "I was told daisies represent love, loyalty and friendship," he tells me, rushing his explanation.

"They do," I whisper, my vision blurring from my tears.

"Don't cry, Pixie. What's wrong?" Reaching out, he cradles my face in his hands, gently brushing my tears away with his thumbs.

Shaking my head, I claim, "Nothing. It's beautiful, Kelly. Thank you, but you didn't have to do this."

He searches my gaze before pressing his soft lips against mine. "I wanted to. Do you want me to put it on?"

Nodding, I force out the words, "Yes, please."

Taking the necklace, he reaches around my neck, hooking the clasp. His fingers skate across my skin, giving me goose bumps. "Beautiful," he murmurs, his gaze focused on me.

I close the distance between us and press my lips to his, moving in a slow, sensual rhythm with my heart thundering against my ribcage. Straddling him, my core burns, feeling his hard length pressed against me. His tongue licks along the seam of my mouth and I gladly open, welcoming him inside. Our tongues collide making me moan as I dive deeper.

His hands fall to my hips, holding me in place and breaking our kiss. "You keep moving like that and it will all be over in seconds," he mumbles over my lips.

Gasping, I arch my back, my nipples straining to get closer to his touch. "I want you, Kelly." I feel his hesitation as he leaves a trail of kisses along my jaw and down my neck, his palm grazing my nipple. "Ahh, please!"

"Are you sure, Pixie?"

"I'm positive. I need to feel every part of you, touching me, kissing me, licking me, fucking me."

Groaning, he stands with my ass in his hands, palming each cheek and carrying me to my room, his lips, never leaving my skin. As he steps over the threshold, I lean back ripping my shirt over my head. "Fuck," he mutters, lowering me to my bed, burying his face in my chest.

Sliding one hand up my back, he unclips my bra, his lips pushing it aside before he sucks my breast into his mouth, flicking my nipple. "Kelly," I whimper, arching towards him, my entire body tingling with desire. "Please, I want to feel you inside me."

His hand slips below my waistband, gliding between my folds and finding my wet heat. "You are ready for me."

Leaning back, I toss my bra to the side and hold his intense stare. "Yes, I am ready for you, Kelly and I don't want to wait anymore."

Rising, he nods, placing his fingers that were just inside me into his mouth and licking them clean. "Mm..." He stands over me, tugging my pants down along with my underwear and dropping them to the floor. A soft hum leaves his lips. "You're so damn beautiful, Pixie."

Fixating on him, I stare as he yanks his shirt over his head, followed by his jeans and boxers, his muscles rippling with each movement igniting me further.

The moment he climbs over me, I wrap my hand around his thick cock making him groan. "Closer."

"Slow down, I need a condom, first."

"In my drawer." I point and he leans over, snatching one out of the nightstand. Ripping it open, he rolls it on making my mouth water before hovering over me once again.

Holding himself above me, he slides his cock between my folds, torturing both of us. Grabbing his ass, I squeeze, arching towards him, his tip at my entrance. "Patience, Pixie. I want to last for you."

"I'm there."

A deep chuckle falls from his mouth. Nipping at my lips, he groans before he devours me whole with a heated kiss. I melt into him, kissing him back with an intensity so deep and pure it's animalistic. Moaning into his mouth, I curve into him, desperate for more.

I feel him at my entrance causing me to beg once again. "Please, Kelly." Slowly, he enters me, pausing for a moment. Then, with one swift thrust he's inside, filling me. "Ah."

Lifting my legs, I wrap them around his back as he moves slowly. "Damn, you feel good, Pixie."

"So do you, but I want more," I rasp, my heels digging into his back. My breathing picks up its pace, our bodies slick with sweat as he moves faster. My body arches towards his meeting every thrust, hitting a spot so deep inside me that my vision starts to blur. "Ah, Kelly. Yes."

Our bodies slap together, echoing against the walls. "That's it, Pixie. I feel you swelling around my dick, so hot and wet. I want to feel you come."

His words do something to me, shoving me over the edge. My head falls back, and my eyes roll back in my head, no longer able to keep them open. "Kelly," I scream his name, unable to remain silent as my core flares, exploding and spreading shockwaves throughout my body while my insides squeeze him, over and over again.

As I'm coming down from my high, his movements become erratic, spurring me on. Rolling his hips, he thrusts deep inside. Grasping my hips, he takes control, chasing his orgasm. Forcing my eyes open, I cling to him, wanting to watch him fall over the cliff.

And then he does and it's so damn sexy.

"Fuck," he groans. Unexpectedly, my insides spasm around him once again while he pulses hitting every wall inside my pussy and I fall along with him, both of us gasping for breath. Plunging into me one more time with a low growl, he collapses on top of me, holding his weight off me.

Taking a deep breath, his voice tickles my neck as he speaks. "Damn, Pixie, I knew you would be everything I need and so much more."

Tears prick my eyes. I press my lips to his chest, my silent appreciation for his heartfelt words.

He kisses me on the top of my head. "Let me go get cleaned up." The minute he slips out of bed, my body shivers, feeling the loss.

Moments later, he's crawling into my bed and pulling me into his strong embrace. "You're back," I whisper, my voice catching, the fact almost overwhelming.

"Are you kicking me out?"

"No."

"Then, I'd like to stay if you'll let me."

In response I wrap my arms around him and lay my head on his chest. Closing my eyes, I breathe him in. I don't want this night to end.

I hear the smile in his voice as he murmurs, "Merry Christmas, Sloane."

Chapter 17

Kelly

The soft curves of her body presses up against mine, my dick instantly aware. My eyes blink open, and I look down at the beautiful woman in my arms. She makes my heart race without even trying. I'm not quite sure how we got here, but I'm sure as hell glad this is where we are.

She shifts, beginning to stir, prompting me to press my lips to the top of her head. "Merry Christmas, beautiful."

I feel her deep breath before she lifts her head, meeting my gaze, a small smile curving her lips. "Good morning." She cuddles closer into my side, my dick getting impossibly harder. "Pixie, we don't have time for me to take you all the ways I want to right now and still get to your mom's for Christmas morning. We slept in. Sorry I kept you up later than I should've."

She groans, the soft vibrations going through me like electricity. "Can't we spend Christmas in bed?"

"I'm not going to argue with that, but will your family?"

She frowns. Lifting her head, she looks at me, her beauty taking my breath away. Her face is clear of makeup, her lips are swollen from our kisses and the pink on her skin is likely whisker burn. I wonder what she looks like between her legs. My eyes flare and I lick my lips, wanting to take her up on her offer, but knowing it's the last thing I should do.

"Are you sure you want to come with me? It's my family, I'll be okay alone."

Holding her gaze, I insist, "I know you will, but I'm coming with you." She smiles and I brush my lips over hers, forcing myself to pull away.

"Oh, wait." She jumps out of bed, taking me by surprise. "I almost forgot, I got you something too." She grabs a large, wrapped package from behind her dresser and a smaller one off the top, setting them down next to me.

She sucks her bottom lip between her teeth prompting me to pull her into my lap and suck her lip into my mouth before my tongue plunges towards hers. She moans, kissing me back, my dick wanting to join but forcing me to slow down. Leaning back, I take a deep breath and lick my lips. "Every time you do that, you drive me wild."

Grinning wide, her eyes sparkle with mischief. "Sorry."

Huffing a laugh, I mumble, "No, you're not." Reaching for the smaller of the two packages, I tear it open. A simple frame with old barn wood encloses a picture of the two of us the night we made our agreement, both of us smiling and glancing at each other out of the corner of our eyes. "You look beautiful. I love it. Thank you."

"It's something to remember me by."

Arching an eyebrow in challenge, I ask, "Remember you? Where do you think you're going?"

She blushes a deep shade of red, veering her eyes away from me. "I just meant because after today, our deal is over."

My heart stutters. "Pixie," I begin reaching for her, but she shakes her head, forcing a smile.

"Not right now, Kelly. We'll talk about it later." I open my mouth to argue, but she stops me once again. "Like you said, we slept late, and I have to get over to my mom's. They'll be waiting for us. You don't have to come, but I have to leave soon either way."

I nod, but I'm not about to let this go.

Pasting a smile on her face, she nudges the larger gift towards me once again. "I hope you like it."

"I know I will," I claim and begin unwrapping. The paper falls away, revealing a large blueprint of the Sagerton place and the grounds with our intended changes. My mouth drops open as I stare at my work mixed with some of hers for the exterior grounds. "Wow. How did you do this? This is incredible."

"You really think so?"

"Yeah, I do. I don't even know what to say."

She shrugs, looking up at me with pride, excitement, and something else I'm not quite sure what it is, but it feels fucking amazing, like I can conquer the world. "I thought it would be fun to see our first project blended together to hang on your wall. I used the plans you gave me. I hope that's okay." Nervously, she sucks her bottom lip into her mouth.

Setting the picture down, I step close to her and cradle her face in my hands. "Yes, it's more than okay. No one has ever done something like this for me before. Thank you for this," I tell her, overwhelmed. My chest tightens. Leaning down, I press my lips to hers, kissing her tenderly, trying to let her know how much this means to me through my lips, but there will never be enough time to show her that. This is incomparable.

Pulling back, I look down at her with the urge to tell her she's stolen my heart. I'm not letting her go, at least not without a fight. But what if she doesn't agree? Will I be able to change her mind? I guess she's right; we need to get through today before we have that conversation.

"Merry Christmas, Kelly."

"Merry Christmas." Grinning, I give her another chaste kiss and pat her ass, playfully. She spins away, laughing as she steps into the bathroom.

That woman has me wrapped around every little piece of her inside and out. I just hope she doesn't want to walk away at the end of our deal because either way, she already carries my heart in the palm of her hand.

Chapter 18

Sloane

The door flies open before we even make it up the steps of my mom's three-bedroom ranch. It was perfect for us after my parents got a divorce, my dad getting Jake and me on Thursdays and every other weekend. Of course, holidays were always shared, and Christmas was always the hardest on me and my brother for two reasons; bouncing from house to house and the memories from the first year when Santa was supposed to be leaving gifts under the tree, but we were left alone and scared instead. After that it was more about blending the families, especially with my dad. He focused more on his new wife and her kids making sure they were comfortable and forgot all about us. For that reason, December has always been difficult for us when all we ever wanted was a happy Christmas.

But this year for the first time, I'm truly looking forward to it because of the man by my side, currently holding an armful of presents.

"Sloane, I'm so glad you're here! Merry Christmas." My mom throws her arms around me and gives me a hug. I barely get my arm around her when she steps back, looking at Kelly with a broad smile. "And you must be Kelly." I'm so happy to meet you. Sloane has told us so much about you."

"She has?" He quirks a brow, glancing at me out of the corner of his eye. "Thank you for having me, Mrs. D–"

"Oh, you can just call me Sharon. I never changed my name after my divorce, and I hate being called Mrs. Douglas." She makes a face. "Come in, come in."

We step inside and I take a step towards the living room, knowing that's where the Christmas tree will be. "You can put those under the tree."

Nodding, he crouches under the tree and sets down the packages, turning back around just as Jake steps into the room with a wide grin. "Howdy, squirt." He steps up to me with his arms wide, pulling me into a hug, my head falling just underneath his chin. He resembles our dad in most ways, unlike me, although he never likes to hear it, their relationship rocky. He's five-feet, eleven-inches with a broad build.

"Merry Christmas, big brother."

"She's a little over the top today," he mumbles a moment before he lets me go and glances at me with his golden eyes, checking to see if I'm okay. I smile up at him, taking a step back as he runs his hand through his light brown hair. He's likely referring to the fact that my mom can go overboard trying to make it up to us at times, especially this time of year. Apparently, this is one of those times.

Shaking it off, I glance at Kelly and introduce them. "This is my boyfriend, Kelly."

Jake grasps Kelly's hand, shaking it firmly before crossing his arms defensively over his chest. "So, you're the Kelly I've heard almost nothing about. In fact, I thought you were a woman until a couple weeks ago."

"Jake," I warn.

Kelly chuckles softly and shrugs. "Yeah, that happens a lot. My name has been both a blessing and a curse," he concedes, giving me a wink. The simple gesture makes me blush.

"How'd you two meet?" Jake asks, narrowing his eyes on Kelly.

My eyes widen, my gaze veering to Kelly as my heart thunders. We never talked about any of this stuff. Isn't that what people normally do in situations like this? Granted, I realize having a fake boyfriend can never be normal, but still–I'm glad he's asking Kelly and not me. Or am I? What is he going to say? He better not mention the bar.

"I come to Genesis Beach often to visit my gram. One of those times, I met Sloane at the flower shop. I stopped there to get something for my grandmother on the way. After that, I kept coming back. Eventually, I got your sister to agree to go out with me. Well, after I told her I was already planning on moving here to be closer to my family."

Jake grins at his sister. "Yeah, her standards include living in a fifty mile radius and treating her right." Chuckling, he claims, "Well, that's partially true. But I'll warn you now, if you ever do something to her like that asshole ex of hers, you'll be looking for more than a new place to live."

Kelly smiles, nodding. "I should hope so. Sounds like you might be as good of a brother as she claims."

Jake laughs, glancing in my direction. "That's true and he's coming to dad's later, right?"

My eyebrows draw down in confusion. "Yeah, why?"

"I want to see that asshole's face when he sees you two together."

"That asshole is dating Fiona."

"Yeah, but I'm pretty sure he's the kind of guy who always wants what he can't have."

"Sloane, will you help me with the food before everyone gets here?" my mom calls from the kitchen.

"Everyone?" Kelly questions.

My eyes widen, realizing I didn't tell Kelly who would be here. "Yeah, my aunts and uncles and a few cousins. My mom was the middle child of five kids. They all come here after they open their presents. We have brunch and then Jake and I leave to go to our dad's and our mom still has family here with her."

"That's really nice."

"Yeah, they're the ones who helped pull her out of her grief and pay some attention to us." Jake winces and I reach out, squeezing his hand. "Sorry, Jake."

"No big deal. Guess he knows?"

"Yeah, he knows everything." The realization hits me as I turn to leave the room. I've never told anyone except Alex everything, and even then, I think there are a few things I left out, yet I confessed my life story to Kelly, the man pretending to be my boyfriend. My stomach twists into knots, a little uneasy that I've trusted him so easily and after today, it might all becoming to an end.

"Are you okay, Sloane?" My mom questions as I step into the kitchen, pulling me out of my darkening thoughts.

"Oh, um, yeah, I was just...let's just say, I'm glad I don't have to worry about you anymore, Mom. You seem happy."

She gives me a genuine smile. "I am sweetheart, I really am."

"Good." I return her grin, grateful things finally feel like they're going in the right direction again for me and my family. I only hope they continue to go in that direction.

Maybe after today is over, Kelly will give me a real chance. At least I hope he will.

Chapter 19

Kelly

Sloane twists her hands in her lap, obviously nervous to walk into her dad's and I fucking hate it. I would give anything to make it easier for her. The moment I park my truck, I reach over, giving her hand a squeeze. "You okay, Pixie?"

"Yeah, I probably should've told you more about everyone before we came."

"Don't worry about me. I can take care of myself. I'm here for you." Leaning in, I give her a chaste kiss.

Jake pulls up beside us, striding right for Sloane's door and opening it for her. "You've got this, Sloane. You have me and Kelly by your side this time unless I have a few too many and start saying stupid shit." He smirks. "Either way, no one else matters, but the two of us."

"Three," she corrects.

"No, I meant what I said. This asshole has to prove himself first. Mom's house was the easy one."

She rolls her eyes dramatically. "Be nice to him. He's here for me."

"True. So, are you ready to take on Christmas?"

Groaning, she agrees, "Fine."

We stride up to the door of a massive modern colonial, just as Sloane's dad opens the door. He smiles. "Oh, good. You're here. We were starting to get worried."

Sloane clenches her jaw and holds my hand a little tighter. Jake forces a smile and mockingly states, "Awe, you were worried about us. That's new."

"Jake," he warns. "It's Christmas."

Jake huffs a laugh. "Don't pretend like that means something to you. Be happy. We're here, ready for this shit show," he mutters stepping around his dad, while his dad sighs, watching Jake.

Sloane shuffles back and forth on her feet. "Um, hi, Dad. Merry Christmas."

Turning back to her, he smiles. "Merry Christmas, Sloane." Her dad leans down, giving her a kiss on the cheek and steps back.

"This is my boyfriend, Kelly."

"It's nice to meet you Mr. Douglas," I claim, holding out my free hand, refusing to let go of Sloane.

He glances at our joined hands before taking my other one and shaking it. "It's nice to meet you. Come on in."

We step inside and he closes the door behind us, just as an older woman with strawberry blonde hair hanging in loose curls steps into the foyer. "Doreen, this is Sloane's boyfriend, Kelly. This is my wife."

"Hello, Mrs. Douglas. Thank you for having me."

She frowns, glancing from me to Sloane, clenching her jaw. "Hi. Your sisters are in the living room waiting. Go say hello."

"Stepsisters," Sloane mutters under her breath, but starts leading me in what I assume is that direction.

The moment we enter the living room, everyone's eyes veer to us. The two women who look a lot like their mother don't look happy to see Sloane, but both their eyes run over me like I'm fresh meat. "Merry Christmas," the first says, smirking. "Is he my Christmas present?"

Leaning towards Sloane, I whisper, "Why does it feel like I just walked back into high school?"

She laughs, quickly covering her mouth.

Forcing a smile, I introduce myself. "I'm Kelly, Sloane's boyfriend."

The woman frowns. "Gia. Nice meeting you."

The other woman steps closer, her eyes narrowed on Sloane. "I know what you're doing Sloane and it's not going to work. You're never getting Daniel back."

Sloane huffs a laugh. "I don't want him back, Fiona. He's all yours."

The man of the hour steps into the room, his gaze instantly drawn to Sloane. Releasing her hand, I slip my arm around her waist, pulling her closer, hating the way the asshole even looks at her.

Jake steps into the room behind him, "Move your gaze, Danny boy. As you can see, she's taken."

He turns his glare on Jake before glancing nervously at the two of us. "Hi, Sloane. Merry Christmas. I remember you. You're Sloane's roommate."

"Boyfriend. Kelly."

"Wait. What do you mean, you remember him? When did you meet him?" Fiona inquires accusingly, crossing her arms over her chest.

He turns beet red and instantly backtracks, making me smirk. "I um, I just ran into them."

"Where?" she challenges, tapping her foot impatiently.

"It's a small town, Fiona."

I huff a laugh, not able to stop it, just as Sloane's dad steps into the room with a drink in his hand. "Alright, everyone. We're family. I know things have not been easy and a lot has changed," he states, glancing between Sloane and Fiona, "but let's try to get along for a few hours. It's Christmas."

"Merry fucking Christmas," Jake mutters under his breath.

"Dinner's ready," her stepmom calls from the kitchen.

Everyone walks in that direction while I hold Sloane in place. "Wait a minute," I request.

Her eyebrows draw down in confusion, but she nods. The moment we're alone she apologizes. "I'm sorry, Kelly, I shouldn't have asked you to come. Jake is right, it is a shit show."

"I don't care about any of that, Sloane. Just tell me, are you okay? Do you want to leave?"

She smiles, her gaze soft. "I'm fine. Thank you. And no, I'll stay. It's only a few hours. Besides, I'm not leaving Jake, especially since he's already had a couple drinks and we've only been here five minutes."

"You're right. He keeps up that pace and he'll need a ride home."

"Thank you, Kelly."

"Stop thanking me, Pixie. I want to be here for you."

"In that case..." She smirks, snaking her arm around my neck and pushing up on her tiptoes, pressing her lips to mine. Her tongue slips into my mouth, a soft moan leaving her lips, and my body reacting.

I weave one hand into her hair, tilting my head and sealing our lips, our mouths moving together making me wish we were anywhere but in her dad's living room.

"Shit," Daniel mumbles, breaking us apart. "Sorry."

"What do you want?" Sloane snaps.

"I just wanted to say I'm sorry."

"You've said that, and I don't care anymore, Dan."

"Sloane," he pleads, trying to stop her as she walks past him.

Stepping in front of him, I block his path, stopping him from chasing after her. "Just some advice. Move on. She has, and you and I both know you weren't man enough to handle a woman as fiery as Sloane. But don't worry, I am, and I take damn good care of her."

Chapter 20

Sloane

Sitting at the dinner table with Kelly on one side and Jake on the other, I feel safe and protected. It shouldn't take the two of them, or either of them for that matter, but my ex took an already shitty situation and made it unbearable. I still have trouble comprehending that he's actually dating Fiona. It definitely makes for messed up family functions. Does it make me a bad person that I hope they crash and burn?

Pushing back from my seat, I say, "Thank you, everything was delicious."

"Are you ready to go?" Kelly whispers.

"We still have to open presents, Sloane," my dad speaks up.

Nodding, I glance at Kelly in reassurance. "I just need to run to the bathroom."

"Okay. Need some help?" he whispers, just loud enough for Dan to overhear, Jake currently too focused on losing himself in his drink. I bite the inside of my cheek to stop myself from laughing. "I'm good."

"Mm..." He hums in appreciation. "Yes you are." Leaning in, he gives me a chaste kiss, goose bumps erupting on my flushed skin.

Standing, I quickly escape to the bathroom, leaning against the white porcelain sink. Taking a deep breath, I let out a harsh exhale and glance at myself in the mirror. The eyes flashing back to me are much brighter than I expected. Whenever I'm around my dad and his family, I'm usually completely on edge. Although, I'm still uncomfortable, I don't seem to care like I have in the past. Is Kelly the reason for the change? Or have I finally moved on from the terrible situation with Dan and Fiona? Admittedly, I think it's a little of both, but it makes me wonder what will happen next time when Kelly is no longer around.

Ready to get the night over with, I push the thoughts out of my head when I know there's no point in worrying about it right now. Turning on the water, I wash my hands. Straightening my shoulders, I slip out the door, startling as I come face to face with Dan. "Oh, sorry about that." I move to step around him, and he slides with me, blocking my path.

"What's the hurry, Sloane?"

I frown. "What do you want?"

"Just give me a minute, please. I want to talk."

"We have nothing to talk about."

"That's where you're wrong. I miss you, baby."

I huff a laugh. "No, you don't. And don't call me baby. You don't like that I moved on or that he's much more of a man than you ever were."

He scoffs, closing the space between us. His body brushes against mine, caging me against the wall. "We were good together. We were planning our life together."

"And you ruined that in an instant." Planting my hands on his chest, I attempt to push him back. "Leave me alone, Dan."

"Please give me another chance. Forgive me, Sloane. I'll make it up to you. I promise."

"I don't give a damn what you do, but it won't be with me. Now, back off," I demand, speaking slow and firm in warning.

"Please," he begs, his lips a breath away, making me turn my head.

"Back up." I push again, but he remains unmoving. Planting my left foot against the floor, I lift my right knee, hard and swift, connecting between his legs.

Instantly, he drops his arms from the wall and keels over, groaning in pain. "Fuck."

Fiona rounds the corner, glaring at me as her eyes drop to Dan. "What did you do?" she screeches.

Out of the corner of my eye, I see everyone in the house spilling into the hallway, following her scream. "I told him to back off and he didn't listen." She glares harder as if blaming me will make the real issue disappear. "Haven't you heard, Fiona? Everyone already knows he's a cheater. But then again, they say that about you too."

Jake laughs. "It's about damn time he got his balls handed to him."

Stepping over Dan, I grin at my brother. Kelly appears just behind him smirking, while the rest of the family stands looking back and forth in shock, unsure what to do. I shake my head and shrug. "It was overdue." Turning to my dad and stepmom, I say, "Thanks for everything, but I think under the circumstances, you can open presents without us this time. Merry Christmas." Grabbing my brother's arm, I urge, "Come on, Jake."

He stumbles, righting himself and laughing. "I'm good. Later," he waves over his shoulder, grinning down at me. The moment we step out the door, he gives me a squeeze. "I'm so damn proud of you."

"Thanks, Jake. Come on, you're riding with us."

He laughs. "Us. You did all right in there, Kelly, but I still don't know about you."

"Thanks, I think," Kelly comments as he helps me get Jake into the back of his truck, just as my dad steps out the front door, his arms loaded with presents.

"Wait!" Turning towards him, I stand, waiting patiently.

"I'm sorry, Sloane. Please, at least take the presents for you and Jake."

Kelly glances in my direction, arching his eyebrow in question. Sighing, I nod. "Sure, Dad. Thanks." Kelly grabs them and puts everything in his truck. I wave, climbing in.

"I really am sorry, Sloane."

"I know, but maybe you could think about the repercussions for other people besides yourself and the family you chose over us sometimes."

"Sloane–"

"Not now, Dad. We're leaving. Merry Christmas."

He pinches his lips tightly together and nods. "Merry Christmas."

I pull the door shut and sink back into the seat.

"You okay?"

"Yeah. Thanks, Kelly."

His lips twitch as he leans towards me. "You know, that was hot as fuck, just please don't ever do that to me."

I laugh. "Don't do anything to warrant me kicking your ass."

"You got it, Pixie."

"Who the fuck is Pixie?" Jake groans from the back seat, already laying down.

Kelly chuckles and gives me a chaste kiss before putting the truck into gear. Pulling onto the road, he turns, heading towards home.

I like having him by my side, even if it is fake. If only this weren't the end of the road for the two of us as a couple.

Chapter 21

Sloane

Taking a deep breath, I settle into Kelly's warm embrace. Questions spin around in my head making me dizzy while we sit staring at our Christmas tree. I'm afraid to open my mouth to ask. Saying the words aloud would make it real, putting me out there hanging by a thread held by him, waiting for him to let it go. Instead, I'm in denial, relishing every moment he'll give me.

Sighing, he kisses the top of my head and runs his hand over my hair and down my arm causing my heart to skip a beat. "How are you doing, Pixie?"

"I'm okay. Thank you for coming with me today and thank you for helping me with Jake. I would've never gotten him home by myself."

"Knowing you, you would've figured it out."

"He dealt with so much more when it came to our parents, always protecting me and probably hiding things from me." I huff a laugh. "He still protects me."

"I can see that. You two are lucky to have each other."

"Yeah," I mumble, sucking my lower lip between my teeth.

Kelly leans over, sucking it gently into his mouth and releasing it, making me laugh. "What's on your mind, Sloane?"

"We've had a busy week."

He nods. "We have."

I press my face into his chest, listening to his heart beat against my cheek. "Now you've seen the chaos of my family."

"And you've seen the madness of mine. What are you trying to say?"

My fingers trace invisible figure eights on his chest, pushing myself to keep going. I have to know. "Well, I guess Christmas is over now, and that means our deal is done too."

His fingers slide underneath my chin, and he nudges it up. "Look at me, please." Taking a deep breath, I lift my head until his intense gaze crashes into mine, holding me captive. "For me, our deal was over a long time ago."

My eyebrows draw down in confusion. "What do you mean?"

"Sloane, I want this, us," he emphasizes. "It didn't take long for you to weave your way into my heart and every part of me and my life. I've been falling in love with you since the day I met you at the bar." He smirks at the memory. "If you think I want to let you go now, you've never been more wrong."

My heart stops before kicking into gear, thrashing against my ribcage. "You're falling in love with me?" I'm barely able to squeak out the words.

He weaves his fingers into my hair and cradles my face in his hands, his eyes never leaving mine. "I'm so in love with you, Sloane and I'm hoping like hell you feel the same way."

I suck in a quick breath, my chest feeling like it's about to burst. "Kelly, I love you, too."

He smiles, taking my breath away. Closing the distance between us, he presses his lips to mine. Starting slow, our mouths move together, finding a perfect rhythm. My body heats as my heart pounds out of control. Snaking my arms over his shoulders and around his neck, I moan onto his lips, the low vibration electrifying our kiss.

His tongue licks along the seam of my lips, begging for entry. Opening for him, our tongues collide, licking, twisting, fighting for dominance, yet I don't care who wins. Tasting him, touching him, kissing him—getting closer is all I want, all I need.

Pulling myself up, I tug on my skirt, lifting it and straddling him. Breaking our kiss, I lean back, pulling my sweater over my head, and tossing it on the floor. Reaching behind my back, I unhook my bra, letting it slide down my arms and dropping it next to my sweater.

"You're so beautiful, Pixie." His hands slide down my body, and around my back. Tugging me towards him, his face falls between my breasts. One hand slips around to the front, finding my nipple, pinching, and twisting. Turning his head, his lips cover my other nipple sucking it into his mouth and flicking it with his tongue.

Groaning, I arch my back, desperate to get closer. My hips buck, grinding over his hard cock, still hidden behind his pants. "Too many clothes."

He chuckles, one hand sliding down as his lips find my other breast, teasing the taut peak with his tongue. His hand glides up my thigh, his thumb running over my heated core. "You're so wet, Pixie. I'm going to make you come, then I'm going to fuck you and make you come again."

His words elicit a whimper, my body curving towards him. Pushing the thin fabric away, his finger dips inside. "Ah, Kelly." Adding a finger, he thrusts, then curls his fingers inside me, while his thumb rubs small circles on my clit. My breathing picks up its pace and my body hums, burning with need.

With one hand on my breast and the other playing my pussy like an instrument, his lips smash into mine with a possessive growl. He kisses me hard, demanding, unrelenting. My head falls back, desperate for breath. His lips fall to my neck, kissing, licking, biting, sucking making me cry out as my body spasms around his fingers, shooting bolts of electricity right through me. "Ah!"

His movements mimic my body's response to his attack, slowing. Removing his fingers, he takes them right to his lips, sucking them clean as he stares at me, his eyes flaring with an impending inferno. "That was the sexiest thing I've ever seen."

My hand slides down his chest flipping the button on his pants. Reaching in, I stroke the length of his cock.

He groans, "Should we take this to the bedroom?"

"No, take me here, right now."

Arching his eyebrows in surprise, he gives me a crooked grin. "You got it, Pixie." I stand up, slowly shimmying out of my skirt and panties while he grabs a condom from his wallet and strips down, rolling it on. Taking me into his arms, he kisses me soft, slow, and demanding, the taste of me on his lips.

Moving my hand between us, I graze his balls and wrap my hand over his hard shaft. Holding it firmly, I slide my hand up and down making him groan. "Fuck, Sloane, I need you."

Grabbing my ass, he lifts me up and I wrap my legs around his back. I grasp his shoulders and with both of us looking between us, I slide down on his cock, both of us groaning at the sensation as he impales me. We hold tight to each other while I move up and down, my tits bouncing with every thrust.

Suddenly, he pulls me close and lowers me to the ground, keeping his hand underneath my head, protecting me when I can't even think. Hovering over me, he takes control, kissing me hard as he plunges deep inside me. My nails dig into his back as my breathing becomes erratic. Pulling back, his lips descend onto my neck, licking, sucking, and nibbling, marking his territory.

"Kelly," I whimper with a fire burning inside me that needs to break free. Skin slapping against skin, grunting, grasping. My insides swell, and with one more hard push of his hips into mine, white flashes in my eyes before darkening. My pussy squeezes his dick, clenching, milking him as we ride out our orgasm together.

"Fuck," he grunts, dragging out the word, his own movements fitful. Breathless, my head falls back as his head drops to my chest. He chuckles, giving each breast a tender kiss. "This is a good place to be."

A smile tugs at my lips. "You're welcome back anytime."

"Anytime?" He arches his eyebrows in challenge making me giggle.

"You know what I mean."

"I do but anytime works for me as long as we can block other assholes from seeing you." I shake my head in amusement, and he gives me a chaste kiss. "I'm sorry, but it looks like I marked you."

"You did, but it's nothing to apologize for. It turned me on even more. Who knew?" I smirk.

He chuckles. "Sounds like we have a lot of things to learn about each other."

"Does that mean you're ready for another round?"

With a broad smile, he kisses me. "Give me half an hour, Pixie, and I'm all yours. Merry Christmas." Licking his lips, he kisses me again, my heart skipping a beat.

"Merry Christmas, Kelly." I grin, my heart full. "Now, this is a Christmas I want to remember."

He chuckles, pressing his face into my neck and inhaling deeply. "I sure won't forget. I love you, Sloane."

"I love you, too."

Standing, he pulls me up with him. "Why don't we take a shower?"

My eyes widen. "Are you saying I stink? Maybe it's because I smell like you," I tease, giddy.

His head falls back as he bursts out laughing. "What am I going to do with you, Pixie?"

"Keep me."

"You got that right." His lips find mine in a heated kiss as he walks me backwards towards the bathroom, happy and content on Christmas for the first time in years.

He's more than I dared to hope for.

Epilogue

Kelly

ix Months Later...

We stand in front of the Sagerton house knowing the finishing touches will be done this week for both the interior and the exterior. Sloane grins from ear to ear. "It looks amazing, doesn't it?"

I nod, not taking my eyes off her. "Yup."

She spins around slowly, taking everything in and then throwing her arms around me once again. "This is so exciting, Kelly! I know you've done stuff like this before, but this is the first project I've seen come to life except when I'm playing around at my mom's house."

"You did an incredible job, Pixie. There will be more jobs to come. Anyone would be lucky to have you."

"Well, it's too bad I'm already taken."

Grinning, I brush my lips across hers. "Yes, you are. Move in with me." I look into her eyes, gaging her reaction.

She smirks, patting my chest, placating me. "Did you forget? We already live together."

"Yeah, we do but your lease is almost up, and my house is almost ready."

Her eyebrows draw down in confusion. "House? What house?"

My lips twitch hopeful and terrified out of my mind. "Our house. I'm the new owner of the Sagerton property."

Her eyes go wide, and her mouth drops open. "What?"

"I didn't know I was going to keep it. For me, it started as a way to move close to my grandmother and then it became a project I loved working on because we got to work together for the first time. Now, it's a place that brought us together and I want it to become our home. I don't want to let go of something that's so important in bringing us together, but mostly, I don't ever want to let go of *you*."

Gulping over the lump in my throat, I remind myself I can do this. I've never wanted anything more in my life. I'm all in when it comes to this woman.

Exhaling slowly, I step back, lowering myself down onto one knee, and pulling a ring out of my pocket. She gasps, her hands instantly covering her mouth in shock. "Kelly."

Holding it up, my hand trembles. I look into her eyes, needing her to know how serious I am about this, her, us. "Pixie, from the moment you came into my life talking about panties and vibrators, I knew I wanted to spend my time helping to drive your passion, for better or worse."

My lips twitch and she huffs a laugh, wiping away her tears. "Oh, my god," she rasps.

"Yes, I like to push your buttons, all of them, and you seem to enjoy pushing mine, but that's part of the reason we're perfect for each other. You know me in ways only you ever will. I love laughing with you, talking with you, working with you, loving you. Now that I know you, spending my life with you is the only way I can imagine it. Move in with me, marry me, be my wife and I will spend the rest of my life making sure you know how truly beautiful and incredible you are. I love you, Sloane. Will you marry me?"

"Yes! Yes, I'll marry you!"

My body relaxes instantly as I stand and wrap her in my arms. Tilting my head down, I cradle her face in my hands and kiss her, my heart beating out of my chest. Leaning back, I whisper, "I love you."

"I love you, too, Kelly."

Pulling back further, I smile so wide my face hurts as I look down at Sloane. "Let me see the ring on your finger."

"You didn't give it to me yet."

"What?" Both of us laugh. Slowly, I roll my hand away from her cheek, the ring falling into my palm. "Oops." Taking the ring, I carefully slip it onto her finger.

"It's so beautiful," she croons, admiring the one carat round diamond with a smaller half carat diamond on each side, all surrounded by an intricate design in a platinum antique setting.

"It was my grandmother's. When I told her I was going to propose she gave it to me. She wanted you to have it and so do I."

Her eyes well, a few tears spilling over her eyelids. She slips her arms around my waist and squeezes tight, pressing her face into my chest. My hand falls to the back of her head. I brush my lips across the top, inhaling her floral scent. "Just please, when you tell her, or anyone about your proposal, don't ever say that you mentioned panties or vibrators."

My head falls back as I burst out laughing. "Anything you want, Pixie. Always."

The End

Acknowledgements

This was such a fun project to be a part of when it first started out with Wreck My Halls and a group of ten amazing authors. Each novella was a spicy, small town story inspired by different Christmas songs. Thank you, Andrea for asking me to be a part of it. I'm thrilled to be able to share my extended version now on my own.

Thank you to my family for your constant support in doing what I'm passionate about. I know I can get in my head, lost in a story sometimes but you are all the most important things in my life.

Thank you, Dina for your help and expertise in editing. Keep asking me the tough questions! I truly appreciate you and what you do.

Thank you to my Street Team, my Beta Team and my ARC Team, I'm so grateful for all you do in helping me get my books out there. It gives me not only the chance, but also the motivation to keep writing. I adore each and every one of you. Thank you to all my readers. I'm more than grateful that I'm able to share my stories with you!

Connect With the Author

Author Website

www.nikkialamersauthor.com

All Author Links

https://linktr.ee/nikkialamersauthor

About the Author

Multi-Award Winning Author, Nikki A Lamers grew up in Wisconsin and lived in Florida for a few years before ending up on Long Island in New York where she now lives with her husband and their two children. Writing, reading, coffee, chocolate, and wine all she needs alongside her friends and family. Since meeting her husband, they enjoy spending time in Maine and exploring different places, meeting new people and always looking for her next story. For her other job she freelances as a script writer, advisor and supervisor on and off set for TV, film and commercials. Now, Nikki is having fun working on her next (several) book(s)!